POLITICAL SCIENCE

A Novel

Jeffrey Seeman

WingSpan Press

POLITICAL SCIENCE
Copyright © by Jeffrey Seeman, 2007
All rights reserved.

This book is a work of fiction. Names, characters, settings and incidents are either the product of the author's imagination or used fictitiously. Any resemblance to actual events, settings or persons, living or dead, is entirely coincidental.

Printed in the United States of America
Published by WingSpan Press, Livermore, CA
www.wingspanpress.com
The WingSpan name, logo and colophon
are the trademarks of WingSpan Publishing.

First Edition 2007

ISBN 978-1-59594-157-2
Library of Congress Control Number: 2007926058

Photo of Jeffrey Seeman courtesy of Craig Damon.

Every nation has the government that it deserves.

– Joseph DeMaistre

AUTHOR'S NOTE

For the record, I want to make clear that the character of Thurmond Stonewall is *not* based on President George W. Bush.

Political Science was actually written in 1993, towards the end of the first Bush administration. At that time, Ann Richards was still governor of Texas and nobody much thought of George W. Bush, the then-president's son. (Of course, there are plenty of people who don't think much of him now, either. But that's a different story.)

When I began circulating this manuscript throughout the publishing industry back in the early nineties, I received lots of praise from various agents and editors, but was repeatedly told the novel was "too controversial" to be published. Instead, I believe the bestselling novel of 1993 turned out to be *The Bridges of Madison County*. You can draw your own conclusions.

So, since I wrote *Political Science* before George W. Bush ever became governor of Texas, the character of Thurmond Stonewall is clearly not based on him.

Besides, the observant reader will note that there are significant differences between Governor Stonewall and President Bush. For example, Governor Stonewall is a Democrat. President Bush, on the other hand, is a Republican. Governor Stonewall is a small-minded, incompetent, unscrupulous reactionary. President Bush, on the other hand, is much taller than he is.

So, as you read *Political Science*, please keep in mind that Thurmond Stonewall was *not* intended as a parody of George W. Bush.

No, seriously.

1/ Austin, Texas, July 4th

What a country.

That's all Governor Thurmond Stonewall could think as he looked out over the flood of people below him—the young couples with children, the teenagers in rock-and-roll T-shirts and cut-off denim jeans, the elderly couples crouched and clinging to each other on the fringes of the crowd. It was a hot afternoon in Austin, dry and in the nineties, as the governor stood on the ceremonial platform that had been hastily erected for the day's festivities. The air was strewn with colorful banners and red, white and blue balloons dotted the sky. Flags hung from every building and the sound of a marching band reverberated in the summer air. There would be a parade that afternoon, followed by the usual ceremonies and speeches, and then a large outdoor barbeque for the citizens of Austin—hamburgers, spicy ribs, sausages heavy with grease. And that night, of course, the traditional fireworks would be seen once again, high above the city skyline, the red and yellow bursts of light exploding outward like flowers opening their petals in those time-lapse films the governor had occasionally seen on National Geographic specials. Governor Stonewall loved Independence Day. The patriotism was so thick in the air he could practically smell it.

What a country.

"Governor, it's almost time for your meeting with Mr. Worthington." One of his secretaries awoke the governor from his reverie.

"Thank you, sweetie pie," winked the governor. "Be right along."

The governor maneuvered his considerable girth across the makeshift stage and down a flight of wooden steps, the planks fairly reverberating under his weight. Who was this Worthington character again? The governor dredged the bottom of his mind for whatever odd details he could find. Someone with a lot of money in Texas oil, as far as he could recall. A big contributor to the last election campaign, but for some reason the governor couldn't remember actually having met the man. Maybe Worthington wanted to ask a favor of him. Sure, he had paid his dues to the governor and now it was time to collect. Or maybe he was going to make another pitch for the governor to run for another term. If that was the case, the governor was ready for him. There was no way anyone was going to talk Thurmond Stonewall out of his retirement.

Stonewall picked his way through the crowd of Independence Day revelers, maneuvering towards the hotel where he had arranged to meet Worthington. It had seemed an odd request, but Worthington's secretary insisted that they meet someplace outside of the state house and that the governor come alone. Stonewall didn't like conducting meetings without his staff there to support him. He relied on them to handle the details while the governor concentrated all his energy on charming whomever his visitor happened to be. But Worthington had been insistent upon the circumstances of the meeting and the governor had learned long ago not to argue with someone of Worthington's wealth. Besides, if anything substantive was transacted, he could always have his staff work out the details later. For the governor's part, he couldn't even remember what the meeting was supposed to be about.

When Thurmond Stonewall had been in college, politics had been the furthest thing from his mind. So, for that matter, had academics. Thurmond had been much more interested in the social life the campus had to offer. He pledged a fraternity his freshman year and quickly became known to his fellow students as an avid partygoer. Rather than studying or becoming involved in campus politics, Thurmond could usually be found at the campus pub, laughing and joking, hoisting a few brews, slapping his fellow fraternity brothers on the backs, and buying a round for the house. He was popular at the state college and gained a reputation for always knowing when and where there was a good time to be had. He could always be counted on to tell you a story or buy you a drink.

After graduation, Thurmond married the woman who had been his college sweetheart. He went on to law school where his academic practices were only slightly more serious than they had been when he was an undergraduate. Eventually he passed the state bar exam and established his own small law practice. And then, surprisingly, Thurmond's years of partying and fraternizing paid off handsomely. For Thurmond had made many friends while in college, more than a few of whom had gone on to play important roles in the state's business community. And when they needed legal work done, it was frequently Thurmond who first came to mind. The serious, conscientious students who had spent their college years studying had probably become better lawyers but, after all, nobody remembered them. Everyone remembered good old Thurmond—good old Thurmond who always had a way with a story and the ladies, good old Thurmond who always knew where there was a party going on. And say, whatever happened to good old Thurmond? He became a lawyer, didn't he? Yes, let's give good old Thurmond a call.

Thurmond's law practice grew rapidly, his legal services in increasingly greater demand. After all, Thurmond may not have been able to quote chapter and verse from the state legal code, but he had lots of friends—judges, prosecutors, even the district attorney himself. Clients hired him not so much for his legal expertise as for his connections and his gift of gab. Thurmond had discovered early on that it was easier to make a man see things your way when he was standing at a bar or a barbeque instead of at the bench, that it was easier to sell him a bill of goods when he was wearing suspenders and shirt sleeves instead of judicial robes. As far as Thurmond was concerned this was a simple fact of nature and he had no qualms whatsoever about taking advantage of it.

And juries loved him. Whenever Thurmond was to appear before a jury he would dress up in his best cowboy finery, complete with spurs on his boots and a ten-gallon hat. A tall man, he'd stride into the courtroom just slightly bow-legged, like he had just climbed down off a horse and was walking into the local saloon for a shot of whiskey. And even at that age he was beginning to put on some weight, so to the casual observer his gait was closer to a waddle than a swagger—a slightly humorous and oddly endearing waddle. And his cheeks would be puffed up like he was holding a full pack of chewing tobacco in each one, his face pudgy as if it had been molded from Play Dough and yet still somehow handsome. And he would dazzle the jury with so much laid-back country charm and down home good humor that they'd have delivered a not guilty verdict to Judas Iscariot himself. Yep, that's what he'd do all right.

As the years went by, Thurmond managed to accumulate a not inconsiderable financial portfolio. This was due only in part to his growing legal practice. The other factor was his well-connected clients, some of the most influential businessmen in Texas. Not that Thurmond would ever have exploited the attorney-client relationship for personal gain. But because he was so well-known and well-trusted, because he was so amiable and good-natured, people just naturally told him things. He couldn't help that, could he? If someone wanted to give him a hot stock tip, he couldn't exactly cover his ears, could he? If, for example, Thurmond had negotiated the divorce of a very well-known and widely respected Dallas oil man, while keeping information about the man's various illicit relationships out of the public eye, and if in exchange for said legal work the man happened to mention that his company was about to acquire a smaller company and that the stocks of said smaller company, currently available for a song, would soon be worth four times as much—well, what was Thurmond expected to do? Bolt from the room at the first word? Pretend not to hear? Admonish this man who had become a trusted friend and was demonstrating his trust by revealing this information? That certainly would have been ungrateful. And if there was one thing Thurmond never was, it was ungrateful.

Thurmond was grateful to his friends for many things. One was the suggestion that he run for governor. "It sure would be nice if one of us was in the state house," a friend had said to him. "Someone who understands the problems of the business community in Texas. Someone like you, Thurmond." At first Thurmond had dismissed the idea. He knew little about politics, cared even less, and harbored a sneaking suspicion that being governor might entail a lot of hard work. But time and again it was suggested to him until the idea seemed to take on a life of its own and Thurmond began to think that just maybe he was the right man for the job after all. He had plenty of popular support, that was for sure. Plenty of friends in high places. A plain-spoken man of the people. A friend to the working man and a friend to business. He was a little of everything, all things to all people, all rolled up into one, that's what he was. Sure, why not? Who better to be governor? The following November, Thurmond ran on the Democratic ticket and handily defeated his opponent.

During his first term if office, Thurmond learned that being governor had its advantages. He enjoyed playing the role of power broker, wheeling and dealing with the state's businesses and unions. He enjoyed the attention, seeing his name in the headlines, being recognized when he walked down the street. And he enjoyed the way people treated him when they wanted something from him. Not that Thurmond had ever accepted a bribe, not really. But if a company or lobby wanted to wine and dine him in order to bend his ear for a few hours, he couldn't exactly refuse, could he? That would be unfriendly, wouldn't it? That could alienate his constituency.

And Thurmond proved to be an immensely popular governor, so much so that now, at the age of sixty-four, he was serving his fourth consecutive term. It was, he had decided, to be his last. He was certainly wealthy enough to retire and spend the rest of his days relaxing on his ranch. The idea of never having to work another day in his life appealed to him. And besides, four terms as governor should be enough for anyone.

The state Democratic Party had tried to convince him otherwise. They knew that, without Thurmond, there was a good chance of the Republicans winning the governor's seat whereas if Thurmond ran again he would almost assuredly be elected for a fifth term. This had nothing to do with his being a good governor. In fact, Texas was in terrible shape—unemployment was at an all-time high, inflation was skyrocketing, companies were going bankrupt or deserting the state in droves, the real estate market had crashed, there was a massive budget deficit, and crime on the streets was rampant. But still, the people of Texas loved Thurmond Stonewall. True, they would never accuse him of being terribly bright, overly honest, or particularly hard-working. But he was one of them and they were mesmerized by his good old boy charisma. Despite all the problems the state had, as the governor neared the end of his fourth term, his favorability rating was at an all-time high.

Yep, what a country.

The brim of the governor's cowboy hat shaded his eyes from the sun's glare, but nothing could save him from its oppressive heat. He mopped his forehead with a handkerchief as he fought his way through the holiday crowd, waving to the many well-wishers who recognized him and bidding them a happy Fourth of July. The smell of exploded firecrackers mixed with that of a thousand charcoal grills and made the governor slightly queasy in the pit of his stomach. The discordant sound of a dozen transistor radios and boom boxes playing a hundred different tunes at once only added to his sense of dislocation. So it was with great relief that he finally arrived at the front entrance of the downtown Austin Hilton and slipped through the revolving door. He was instantly doused with cool air from the main lobby.

The governor took the express elevator to the top floor of the hotel and got off at the Armadillo Lounge. It was an elegant bar with plush carpeting and enormous floor-to-ceiling windows that allowed one to look out over the city skyline. Small sculptures of armadillos were placed here and there, presumably to justify the establishment's name and to remind tourists that they were in fact in Texas and not New York. In honor of the holiday, red, white and blue festoons had been placed above the doorway. All very tastefully done, the governor thought.

"Say there, pretty thing." The governor caught the eye of one of the waitresses. "Know where I can find the Worthington party?"

"Yes sir, Governor," she replied, flustered as if she had just met a movie star. She directed him to a table on the far side of the room.

As the governor approached the table, he noticed a middle-aged man seated there with two boys. The boys were maybe sixteen years old and looked close enough alike to be twins, both with short, well-groomed hair and dark good looks. They were both precisely dressed in what appeared to be very expensive, hand-tailored suits. As for the man, he was dressed quite a bit more shabbily, in a rumpled grey suit that certainly hadn't put a dent in anyone's bank account. A father who cares more for his sons than himself, perhaps? A contributor who promised the boys he'd take them to meet the governor? But no, that wasn't quite right. The governor couldn't quite get a handle on it.

"Mr. Worthington," he said as he reached the table, extending his hand towards the man in the grey suit.

The man barely looked up from his whiskey. "Not me," he said. He shrugged towards the boys.

"Governor Stonewall. So pleased to make your acquaintance, sir." One of the boys stood and shook his hand. "Allow me to introduce myself. I am Reginald Myers Worthington and this is my brother, Bret." The other boy also stood and the governor, dazed, shook his hand as well. What the hell was going on? Who were these kids?

"And this is our associate, Joel Heidelman," said Bret. "You can call him Scoop. Everyone else does."

"Charmed," said Scoop, barely acknowledging the governor's presence.

"Please be seated," Reginald motioned to the governor. Dumbly, fearing he was being made a fool of, the governor obeyed. He glanced towards the only other adult at the table for some sort of explanation, but Scoop continued to evade his glance. Were these teenagers going to be conducting the meeting? Was this someone's idea of a joke? Collecting his wits, the governor tried to regain the initiative.

"Well, it's a real pleasure to meet you boys. Is your dad going to be along soon?"

A bemused smile crossed Reginald's face. "If he did, it would be quite a surprise. He's been dead for some years now, you see. I apologize for causing you confusion, Governor. Of course, you can't be faulted for jumping to the obvious assumptions. But we aren't expecting anyone else at this meeting. I am the Mr. Worthington with whom you were scheduled to meet this afternoon."

The governor's eyes passed from Reginald to Bret to Scoop and back again. "Listen, son, it's been right nice to meet you. I always have said that the future of Texas rests with its young people. But I'm a very busy man, son. So if you'll excuse me…" The governor rose to go.

"Sit down, Governor," said Reginald. There was something commanding in his voice, something not at all childlike. Instinctively, the governor obeyed.

"I realize how this must look to you," Reginald continued after the governor settled back into his chair. "But my brother and I have both been generous contributors to your last two campaigns and I believe that entitles us to at least get a hearing from you. I'm sure there must be many questions going through your mind right now. Let me try to answer some of them by telling you a little about my brother and myself. That way we can dispense with this ridiculous parent-child dynamic and get down to the matter at hand.

"My brother and I are, in fact, twins. We are sixteen years of age.

I graduated from Princeton at the age of ten with a degree in political science. I then attended Oxford as a Rhodes Scholar, where I wrote a thesis on the future of the two-party system in the U.S. and its relation to socio-economic stratification. I received my doctorate at the age of twelve. I speak seven languages, including Russian and Hebrew. For the past several years, I have been working behind the scenes of several Congressional campaigns, offering them the benefit of my knowledge and expertise.

"My brother Bret, on the other hand, found his fascination in the world of business rather than politics. He graduated from the Harvard Business School with an MBA at the age of eleven. For the past few years he has been one of the leading brokers on Wall Street, managing the justifiably famous Capital Appreciation fund for the firm of Lerner and Stein. He recently resigned from that position to start his own software company, write his autobiography, and pursue other interests.

"Each of us received a hefty inheritance upon our father's death and, owing to astute business dealings and investments, we have managed to more than triple our assets. My brother and I now have a combined portfolio worth over $100 million. We frequently use said finances to make contributions to political campaigns of our choosing, of which yours was recently one.

"I would appreciate being called Reginald. My brother answers to Bret. Please do not address me as 'son.' Neither of us is your son and of this we are both quite certain. Now that we've gotten all that out of the way, let's get down to business. Would anyone care for a drink?"

Reginald motioned to one of the waitresses. She approached the table immediately, a trimly uniformed woman with frizzy red hair. "I'm afraid I can't serve you alcohol without an ID," she explained politely.

"Of course you can't, my good woman," said Reginald, "nor would we think of asking you to do anything that would jeopardize the reputation of this fine establishment. I will therefore have a Perrier with a twist of lime. My brother here will have the same. Please get our associate another scotch on the rocks. And you, Governor?"

The governor's head was still spinning. "Bourbon," he managed to blurt.

"Bourbon," repeated Reginald. "Your finest, please. And," he added, noticing the dazed look in the governor's eyes, "perhaps you should make that a double."

After everyone was settled with their drinks, Reginald turned to the main order of business.

"Governor," he began, "we are here to talk to you about running for office."

At last, thought the governor. Something that wasn't completely unexpected. Something to which he knew how to respond.

"Sorry, boys, but you should have said that to begin with. I could have stopped you right then and there and told you you were wasting your time." The governor took a long sip of bourbon and felt the liquor warm the back of his throat. "See, at the end of this term, I'm retiring. I'm pulling up my stakes and moving out. That's it. Ain't nothing no one can say to change my mind. This is my last term as governor."

"But we're not here to talk to you about running for governor," said Reginald. "We're here to talk to you about running for president."

The words sent an almost electric shiver through the governor's large body. Surely he had never confessed such ambition to anyone, not even to his wife. Yet there were times, moments of vanity and glorious self-delusion, when he had been surprised to find the idea lurking in the back of his mind. And here was this boy actually saying it out loud, without a hint of sarcasm or jest. In that split second the governor could picture himself—in the White House, greeting heads of state, riding down Pennsylvania Avenue in a long black limousine, crowds of admirers shouting his name... "Stonewall! Stonewall! Stonewall!"

"Just, uh...just what makes you think I'm your man? I mean, why me?" It was a question prompted more by a desire to be flattered than by any particular sense of modesty.

Reginald shrugged and gulped his Perrier. "You have a history of being an excellent fund-raiser."

"Yes," echoed Bret, "an excellent fund-raiser."

"Oh." The governor had expected something more lofty, but he wasn't sure what. Maybe something about his intellect or his leadership capabilities.

"Yes, you've raised a hefty amount during your last three gubernatorial campaigns," continued Reginald.

"A hefty amount," said Bret.

"Yes, I reckon that's so," said the governor.

"I'll bet," said Reginald, and he leaned forward over the table to look the governor in the eye, "I'll bet there have even been some campaigns where you've raised more money than you've actually spent. Isn't that so, Governor?"

"Sure," shrugged the governor. "It happens,"

"And where does that money go? I mean, the money that isn't spent."

"Into my war chest. You know, I hold it over till the next election like everyone else. Why?"

"Nothing," said Reginald. "Nothing at all." He leaned back in his seat. "And do you have any idea how much you'd be able to raise if you declared yourself as a candidate for president?"

The governor shrugged. "Never gave it much thought. A few million, I suppose."

"Eight million dollars in the first four months, according to my calculations," said Bret. "Give or take a few hundred thousand." He smiled like a precocious child trying to impress an adult which, the governor realized, was precisely what he was.

The governor shifted uncomfortably in his chair. Somehow the conversation had gone from the tantalizing idea of himself as president to some minutiae about campaign finances. "So, you boys really think I could get elected president?" he asked, trying to get things back on track.

Reginald smiled in a way that was almost condescending, almost cruel. "Frankly, Governor, no. According to our research, your appeal is strictly regional. You have little name recognition outside the Western states. Northerners wouldn't have a clue what to make of you. To be perfectly blunt, you haven't got a prayer of getting elected."

Reginald might just as well have thrown his drink in the governor's face. The governor fairly jolted in his seat, as if he were a prisoner strapped into the electric chair and they had just switched on the juice.

"What the…what the hell is this all about then?" he demanded.

Reginald studied his Perrier. "What this is all about, Governor, is simply this. The fact is, it is possible for one to raise more money in a campaign than he spends, is it not? You yourself just said as much. It happens all the time."

The governor shrugged. "Well, what about it?"

"Well," said Reginald, "hasn't that money ever tempted you? I mean, it would tempt anyone, don't you think? It would only be human. Haven't you ever thought about using that money for something else? Something other than the next election, I mean?"

"Like what?" asked the governor.

"Like your retirement, for example. After all, you've devoted many years to serving the public. Now, at the time of your retirement, you're entitled to a little bonus, don't you think? I mean, you would certainly get as much if you had served in the private sector. Why should you be denied that because you chose to dedicate your life to public service?"

The governor squinted, not sure of what he was hearing. "Are you saying I should take the excess from my last campaign? I can't do that! That money's earmarked for the Texas Democratic Party, for God's sake! I can't..."

Reginald raised his hand to cut off the speech. "With all due respect, Governor, I'm afraid you still haven't quite got it. We're not talking about the measly contributions from some past gubernatorial campaign. We're talking about the far more substantial contributions to a possible future presidential campaign."

There was a long moment of silence during which the realization leapt forth into the governor's mind, a thousand wild thoughts chasing after it. Finally, he slammed his drink down on the table.

"Of all the goddamn, stupid, idiotic... What the hell are you thinking, boy? Are you completely out of your goddamn mind? You can't count on making money on an election campaign, for Christ's sake! What the hell is wrong with you? That kind of thing happens once in a while as a fluke, for Christ's sake! A goddamn fluke! What the hell did you think? That you could set it up like some kind of goddamn investment? Of all the stupid, asinine... You act like a real hot shit, a real smart-ass kid, and then you go and say something so totally goddamn foolish. Well, Jesus H. Christ, I'm gonna let you in on a little secret, boy. It costs one hell of a lot of money to run a campaign in this country!"

Reginald smiled, completely unfazed. "No," he corrected, "it costs a lot of money to run a *winning* campaign. What if the whole point of the campaign is to lose?"

"To lose?"

"Think about it. The reason campaigns cost so much is because you're trying to win. What if you weren't? What if you spread just enough money around to make it look good and then pocketed the rest? All you'd have to do is make sure you spend less money than you raise. If you were to raise, say, eight million dollars and spend only two million...well, that would leave quite a profit, don't you think?"

"Quite a profit," said Bret.

The governor sat dumbly for a moment while the possibilities raced through his mind. He pretended to concentrate on his drink, taking several long, slow sips, the liquor now partially diluted by the melting ice cubes. By the time he lowered the glass back onto the table it was empty and a gentle smile had found its way onto his face.

"Well, I reckon I've heard just about everything now," the governor said. "Got to hand it to you boys. I thought I'd heard it all, but this sure is a new one on me. Why I feel like a cow who's just had her first dance with a milking machine."

"Please, Governor," said Reginald, not unkindly, "save the hayseed routine for the voters. It's really quite unnecessary with us."

"Quite unnecessary," said Bret.

Instantly, the governor's smile disappeared. "Okay, you boys want to talk straight, I'll talk straight." He pulled his chair up close to the table. "Now I'm not saying I'm interested or anything, but just supposing I was. There's at least a jug-full of reasons I can think of why your idea hasn't got a chance in hell of working."

"Really?" said Reginald, vaguely amused, "Okay, Governor. I'm game. Shoot."

"First off is the obvious. Campaign finances are carefully monitored by the FEC. There's no way I could use any donations made to my political campaign for personal gain. Not without getting my hand caught in the cookie jar, if you know what I mean."

"We can handle that," said Reginald. "Suffice it to say that to most people accounting is the most mundane of sciences. In the hands of my brother, however, it is an art form. There's nothing that can't be accomplished with a little creative bookkeeping. What else?"

"Okay, what about this? During an election campaign—particularly a presidential election campaign—everyone is watching everyone else like a bunch of goddamn vultures waiting for something to die. All the candidates are trying to dig up dirt on all the other candidates and the press is trying to get dirt on everyone. That's how the game is played. You get enough dirt on a guy, you knock him out of the race. Now in the middle of all that you claim you're gonna raise eight million dollars and spend only two million and you don't expect anyone to notice?"

"That's absolutely right," said Reginald, "They won't notice because you'll be losing, remember? You think the other candidates are going to bother trying to sabotage a campaign that's already going down the tubes? You think the press is going to run stories on a candidate no one cares about? People pay attention to winners, Governor. They'll be putting the front runner under a microscope, not the dark horse at the back of the pack. And when the campaign is over and you slink back into national obscurity, no one will even remember you. No one will guess you've actually turned a profit, no one's going to look over your shoulder, and no one's going to bother checking your books because you're a loser and nobody pays attention to losers. Honestly, now. Can you name the first candidate to drop out of the last presidential race? Of course not. No one can. No one remembers." Reginald smiled. "No one cares."

The governor thought silently for a moment. "All right," he conceded, "you may have something there. But answer me this. If this is such an airtight little scheme, how come no one's ever tried it before?"

Reginald and Bret exchanged mischievous glances. "What makes you think no one has?" said Bret.

The governor's eyes grew wide with wonder. "You sons of bitches... You saying you've already pulled this off?"

The brothers broke into identical boyish grins, looking for all the world like a pair of normal teenagers who had just been caught in some high school prank, soaping the principal's car windows or peeking in the girls' locker room. "Well, obviously we couldn't possibly say," said Reginald.

"Couldn't possibly," said Bret.

The governor scratched his head, his hair still slightly damp from sweat. The more they talked, the less crazy the idea began to seem. The governor was already a wealthy man, but eight million dollars was an awful lot of money. It could certainly make his retirement just a little more comfortable.

"Okay, I'll tell you what," he said finally. "Now I'm still not saying I'm interested or anything. But if I were—just hypothetically speaking—what exactly are you proposing? I mean, I don't know jack shit about national politics or running a presidential campaign or any of that."

"We can handle that," said Reginald. "I would serve as your campaign manager, my brother Bret as your finance chairman, and our friend Scoop here as press secretary. We have all served in these roles during previous Senate and Congressional campaigns. My brother and I will provide the seed money to set up the operation. We concentrate principally on the four big money states—New York, Texas, Illinois, California. After you drop out of the race, we get back the return on our original investment. Any money in excess of the initial start-up costs are split, seventy-thirty."

"Why seventy-thirty?"

"It's only fair. It's our money that's bankrolling you."

"But it's my career that's on the line."

"You're career is over one way or the other, isn't it?"

"But it's my reputation," the governor insisted. "It's my good name."

Reginald folded his hands on the table before him. "These are minor details. I'm sure we could work them out in the future, if that proves necessary. The important thing for now is that you think about our proposal. Go on home, talk it over with your wife. Kick it around. Give us a ring when you've reached a decision."

"When you've reached a decision," said Bret.

"Uh-huh," said the governor. He squinted and shook his head slowly. "You realize this whole crazy plan of yours is illegal about ten different ways."

"Well, yes," said Reginald. "I suppose that's so."

"Doesn't that bother you?" said the governor. "Not even just a little bit?"

"No," said Reginald, perplexed. "Why should it?"

The governor lowered his voice and leaned forward slightly. "Well, what if someone catches on?"

Reginald smiled. "No one has yet."

2/ Texas, September 25th

The telephone rang in Scoop's hotel room at a little after eight in the morning. Scoop picked it up on the fifth ring.

"Scoop, this is Reg. Did I wake you?"

"Naw. I was already on my second bourbon."

"Bourbon? Why are you drinking bourbon at eight o'clock in the morning?"

"I was out of scotch."

"Oh. Listen, Earl's got the final cut of the TV commercial. We're meeting at nine in my room to watch it."

"Gotcha."

Scoop hung up the phone and settled back in bed. He rested his glass in the carpet of hair on his chest and stared absently into the amber liquid. The morning light was prying its way through the curtains, casting reflections on the rim of the glass and sending spindly white fingers across the floor of the room, strewn as it was with clothes, newspapers, notebooks, empty cans of Coke, and the white cardboard carcasses of half-eaten Chinese food. Scoop felt a dull pain in the pit of his stomach that might have been the bourbon or might have been the lo mein. Or maybe it was just the resentment of waking up again in this crummy hotel room in the middle of godforsaken Texas. Texas, where on a cool day the temperature might only reach ninety-five. Texas, where their idea of culture was drinking a six-pack of Budweiser and watching a tractor pull on the Nashville Network. Texas, where all the pick-up trucks had gun racks and bumper stickers with pithy sayings like "Keep On Truckin' For Jesus." Texas, home of the brave. Texas, where the deer and the antelope play. Texas, kiss my fucking ass.

Not that Scoop had anyplace else he particularly wanted to be. He was what was charitably referred to as a "political consultant" and uncharitably as a "hired gun." His life was an on-going series of election campaigns—presidential, of course, but also Senate, Congressional, gubernatorial, wherever the action was. He lived from election day to election day and when one campaign ended he simply hopped aboard the next one leaving the station. His specialty was handling the press—getting coverage for his candidate, putting the best possible slant on news events, putting the best possible spin on his candidate's inevitable gaffes. For this he was handsomely paid. He had spent the vast majority of his adult life at press conferences and fundraisers, in airports and hotel lounges and smoke-filled rooms, rubbing elbows with lobbyists and reporters and assorted party hacks, drinking too much, eating in bad restaurants and staying up far later than any human being should reasonably be expected to. The physical impact this had had on him was obvious. Once trim and healthy, he was now paunchy and walked with a slight stoop. The late hours had produced permanent bags under his eyes and he had a hacking cough that came and went, the result of inhaling years' worth of second-hand smoke.

Scoop had become interested in politics while studying journalism in college. It was 1964 and the first seeds of political activism were beginning to take root in campuses across the nation. To students in those days, the initials CD stood for "civil disobedience," not "compact disc" or, worse yet, "certificate of deposit." Scoop became active first in the civil rights movement and then in the anti-war movement. He attended rallies, distributed leaflets, participated in demonstrations—even squeezed in the occasional class when his schedule allowed. By the time he was a senior, he was a member of the Committee of Concerned Democrats and organizing for Eugene McCarthy, who was seeking the Democratic nomination on an anti-war platform. To Scoop, McCarthy was a larger-than-life hero, a true patriot who would lead America away from war and racism and back to the original ideals put forth by Thomas Jefferson—justice, freedom, equality. Scoop threw himself into the campaign with a passion the likes of which he had never before experienced. The walls of his dorm room were strewn with antiwar slogans and McCarthy campaign posters.

Then came 1968. It became clear that Vice President Hubert Humphrey, the establishment candidate, had a lock on the presidential nomination and the Democratic convention exploded into violence on the streets of Chicago. Scoop witnessed the brutality first-hand, thousands of young people being clubbed by Mayor Daly's police force as clouds of tear gas rose like steam in the streets, clawing at his eyes and forcing vomit into the back of his throat. It was a shock to Scoop's youthful idealism, a slap of sobering reality. He had seen the country he loved reduced to the level of a brutal, two-bit dictatorship, ruthlessly choking off the cries of the people who, in Scoop's mind, were trying to save it.

But if the events of 1968 stunned him, they did nothing to quell Scoop's enthusiasm for the political process. To the contrary, he became convinced more than ever that the system was in need of reform, of a new broom to sweep clean. The problem with McCarthy, Scoop decided, was that he was never really a viable candidate. He had been in the race to raise issues, not to win. So, with a newfound pragmatism, Scoop turned his attention towards the future and a candidate whom he felt actually had a shot at the White House. That candidate was George McGovern.

Scoop was drafted by McGovern's campaign coordinator Gary Hart, then a 34-year-old Denver lawyer. He worked as a grass-roots organizer, driving back and forth across the Midwest, compiling lists of potential McGovern supporters, making phone calls, holding meetings in people's living rooms and barns, putting together a network of volunteers. When McGovern won the nomination of his party in July of 1972, Scoop felt vindicated at last. The month before had brought the first word of the Watergate break-in and the Nixon campaign had been tainted with scandal. To Scoop, it was only fitting, serving to place the two candidates in even greater contrast— McGovern, the bold idealist with fresh new ideas about peace and equal rights, and Nixon, the venal backroom politician, protector of the corrupt status quo. The choice couldn't have been more clearly delineated nor the contest more crucial.

And of course, in November, the American people made that choice. It was almost too much for Scoop to comprehend. He sat alone in a hotel room in South Dakota, unable to face anyone, the room completely black except for the flickering light from the television screen casting electromagnetic shadows across the floor as the election results came in. How could it have happened? For the American people to be given such a clear-cut choice and to have chosen so poorly—how was it possible? Not only to lose, but to lose in the greatest landslide in U.S. history. And then McGovern himself was there on the screen, there in that very hotel room, and he was conceding the election to Nixon and it was over. And Scoop's eyes were red with tears and he finished a fifth of Cutty Sark all by himself that night. He remembered a government professor he had had in college who said that every country gets the leadership it deserves. The liquor tasted stale and harsh in Scoop's mouth.

After that, he drifted from campaign to campaign. He was still quite adept at his job and even began learning to use his training in journalism to his advantage when dealing with the press. But his heart wasn't in it any longer. He didn't care much who won or lost, where the candidates stood on the issues or what they were saying. They all started to sound alike after awhile anyway. And what was the point? The issues really didn't have much to do with the democratic process. The more campaigns Scoop worked on, the more he realized that. Campaigns were just popularity contests where the candidate with the most money won. They were childish battles of name-calling and finger-pointing, gossip and innuendo, where each candidate slung mud at the other and the press took bets on how much would stick to each. They were advertising campaigns of style over substance and image over issues, where a candidate's personality was more widely discussed than his intelligence and his slogans were far more important than his ideas. They were a form of entertainment, a road show with carefully orchestrated photo ops and sound bytes, perfectly packaged for easy consumption on television news shows, where they would be sandwiched between advertisements for tampons and the latest diet soft drink. None of which served to determine who the best person for the job was or in any way facilitate his ascension to office, of course. In short, Scoop had seen the inside of American democracy and it didn't work.

Given the prevalent moral climate, Scoop felt no compunction about becoming what was essentially a political mercenary. Work for a right-wing Republican in New England? Sure. A racist Congressman from South Carolina? Why not? What did it matter, anyway? Same shit, different wrapper.

It was during a particularly dirty Senate race that Scoop first met the Worthington brothers. They had heard of his agility in handling the press and had offered him a position on what they referred to as their "team." They described to him a rather far-fetched idea they had, to use the political process itself as a means of turning a profit. Scoop found the idea intriguing and signed on. They started small with a state Senate race out in Arkansas, learning the limits of the scheme, how far they could push the profit margin before anyone caught on. From there they worked their way up to a gubernatorial race and a U. S. Senate campaign. And now they were ready for the big time: the presidency.

Of course, Scoop was well paid for his services. The Worthingtons always cut him in on a share of the profit. But to Scoop, the main appeal of the Worthingtons' scheme was not financial. Rather, Scoop enjoyed the poetic justice of it all, the way the entire complex political process could be manipulated towards such a simple goal, a goal that was in many ways much purer than most of those in politics. After all, most political players were steeped in hypocrisy, always claiming they were interested in the public good, but secretly operating with a hidden agenda formed by a desire for personal gain. The Worthingtons, on the other hand, were completely honest in their motives. They wanted money, lots of money, as much as they could get. Scoop found something refreshing about this unabashed form of greed. And why not? The democratic process was a moral vacuum, a wasteland of ignorance and corruption, a sideshow of arrogance and the lust for power. Why not exploit it to make a quick buck? To Scoop, there was something fitting in that.

As for the money, Scoop had little need for it. He spent most of his life in hotel rooms, living off campaign expense accounts. He never took vacations and couldn't even imagine himself living a life different from the one he led. He had no future ambitions and no plans to settle down. At the age of fifty-three, he had no wife and no family to speak of. If pressed, he would inform you that politics was his mistress and his only love, though in truth the love had long since gone out of the relationship and all that was left now was a sort of detached screwing.

By the time Scoop showered, shaved, and got to Reginald's hotel room, the lights had already been dimmed and Earl Jeeter, the campaign's head of public relations, was force-feeding a videocassette to the VCR. Jeeter was a perpetually nervous man with small, shifty eyes and an expansive forehead that always looked as if it threatened to slip down over the rest of his face. He also had a habit of biting his lower lip, which Scoop found particularly annoying. Scoop disliked Jeeter, but no more so than he disliked anyone else.

"Nice of you to join us, Scoop," said Reginald with only a hint of sarcasm. He, Bret, and the governor were seated on a couch facing the television, while other staff members sat on chairs scattered about the room. Scoop shrugged off the comment and made his way to the coffee machine, which was always kept replenished, twenty-four hours a day. Reginald's room was identical to Scoop's—same tacky peach carpeting and uncomfortable walnut furniture, same generic paintings on the walls. In fact, the only difference was that the hotel maids didn't draw straws to see who would have to clean Reginald's room. Scoop poured himself a cup of black coffee and leaned back against the far wall opposite the television.

He had seen the governor's kind a thousand times before—self-important politicians bloated with rhetoric and enamored of their own dubious charm, two-bit con artists greedy for their shot at the big time. He could see right through the governor's "aw shucks" façade, the country warmth and folksy humor, straight through to the slick manipulation beneath, like lifting up a rock and seeing what slime crawled below, and it amazed him that the voters evidently couldn't see it as well. Couldn't or wouldn't, Scoop was never sure which. Americans seemed to enjoy deluding themselves. Hungry for heroes, they would wantonly embrace the faintest imitation—the soap opera star, the quarterback, the young rapper fresh from his first MTV video—and lavish them with the kind of praise and adoration that in older societies had been reserved for royalty. It was an idiotic way to establish celebrity, never mind leadership. Scoop idly wondered if the governor had any inkling of what the lives of his constituents were really like. Had he ever left his ranch and driven into the slums of the cities? Had he ever listened to the complaints of the unemployed or looked into the faces of the homeless? Scoop didn't think so. This was a man obsessed with himself, a man who reduced every political equation to a simple question of self-interest.

Well, what the fuck. Doubtless he'd be no worse than anyone else on the ballot.

"Before we begin," said Bret, "let me remind everyone that low overhead means high profits. The idea is to take in more money than we spend and, therefore, to keep expenses as low as possible. For that reason, some corners may have been cut in the filming of this commercial, so long as they did not adversely affect the overall quality of the finished product. Go ahead, Earl."

The television screen turned to static for a moment, then black. And then the first strains of "America, the Beautiful" were heard as a grainy, slightly out-of-focus image of the American flag filled the screen. An off-screen announcer began talking, but the sound quality was so poor it was difficult to make out exactly what he was saying. The announcer seemed to have a bad head cold, or maybe just a large amount of mashed potatoes shoved in his mouth. He made a reference to "the future of our nation," or maybe it was "the fuchsia fornication," it was hard to tell. The background music fluttered, struggling to stay at a consistent speed as if someone was dragging his elbow over the turntable while the record played.

"Here it comes," prompted Bret.

Suddenly the governor was on screen, walking through a factory, shaking hands with people on the assembly line. The image seemed jittery, as if it had been taken by a nervous cameraman with a hand-held camera, and the picture veered drunkenly in and out of focus. Every so often the camera would take an unexpected leap upwards towards the ceiling or down towards the governor's shoes.

"Nice shoes," said Scoop.

"Shhh," said Bret.

Then the governor was shown outside a supermarket talking to consumers, a concerned look on his face, while the announcer talked about "the cost of living" or "the cost of liver" or something like that. Then a shot of the governor and his wife walking hand-in-hand through an oil field. Pat, the governor's wife, was dressed simply, smiling, a vacant expression glued to her face. Scoop had met her on several occasions and had reached the conclusion that the only distinguishing aspect of her personality was her complete lack of one.

Finally the image of the American flag was back on screen, but this time with the governor standing before it, looking resolutely into the camera. The music built to a crescendo and the picture faded.

"Well, that's it," said Bret, leaping up to turn the lights back on. "What do you think?"

"What the…what the hell *was* that?" demanded the governor.

Bret seemed genuinely surprised. "You didn't like it?"

"Like it? I didn't even *understand* it, half the time! It looks like it was made by a goddamn eight year old!"

"As a matter of fact," said Reginald, "I'll have you know this commercial was directed by one of the finest adult filmmakers in Austin."

"One of the finest," said Bret.

"I don't give a good goddamn if it was directed by Steven fucking Spielberg," said the governor. "The picture was all blurry. The camera kept jumping around."

"Actually, that's considered very 'in' these days," said Reginald. "You know, commercials filmed with a hand-held camera, images not quite in focus. It's very hip, very avant-garde."

"Very *cinéma vérité*," said Bret.

"Cinnamon *what*?"

"What did you think of it, Scoop?" asked Reginald.

Scoop shrugged. "Could've been worse, I guess. Could've left the lens cap on."

"Look, trust us on this," Bret said to the governor. "It'll be fine. Really. Have we steered you wrong yet?"

The governor scowled. "Damn campaign ain't even started," he muttered, half to himself. "Haven't had a goddamn *chance* to steer me wrong yet."

"Good, then it's settled," said Reginald. "We'll run with this commercial. Good job, Earl. Bret, what's our bottom line look like?"

"Exceptional," his brother replied. "Contributions to the Committee For a New America have been even better than projected. We established the political action committee, of course, to get around the FEC regulations. As long as the governor isn't a declared candidate, we can continue to insist that the Committee isn't a campaign fund and therefore that the FEC limits on campaign contributions aren't applicable. As a result, we've managed to raise close to two million dollars in just two months, mostly through corporate contributions from Texas and nearby states."

"Excellent," said Reginald. "And do you think we should continue to hold out?"

Bret leaned back into the sofa and absently fingered a mechanical pencil. "Well, that's really the sticky question, isn't it? I mean, the longer we remain undeclared, the longer we can use the Committee as a front, which grants us a tremendous amount of freedom. On the other hand, there's been a flurry of candidates throwing their hats into the ring lately. And once he's declared, a candidate can go right to the people for donations. I'd hate to think those other campaigns may be siphoning off contributions that would be ours if we were in the race officially."

"So what does that mean?" asked the governor, leaning forward impatiently. "What do we do?"

Bret rose to refill his coffee cup. "I think it's time to drop the subterfuge," he said. "I think we should declare. What do you think, Reg?"

"I agree. The timing feels right. Scoop?"

"Why not?" said Scoop. "Let's do it already. The suspense is killing me."

"Earl?"

"No objection from me."

"We're agreed then," said Reginald. "Earl, file the necessary papers. Scoop, call a press conference for tomorrow. Late afternoon, so we can make the evening news."

"Check," said Scoop.

"Hot damn," said the governor. "This is more like it. We're finally gonna do something! Just let me at the poor suckers. They won't know what hit 'em. They won't have a prayer in hell." The governor lifted his coffee cup into the air like a beer mug. "To the campaign."

"And may the best man lose," added Bret, lifting his cup as well.

From around the room, cups of ceramic and Styrofoam were hoisted in half-serious salute.

"Gentlemen," concluded Reginald, "let's make some money."

So, late on the afternoon of September 26th, a press conference was convened on the steps of the state capitol. It was like the Fourth of July all over again, like an explosion in a flag factory. A brass band from a local high school played marching tunes off-key, balloons filled the sky and patriotic banners hung everywhere. Mimicking the image from the soon-to-be-released television commercial, the governor stood before a large American flag and delivered a short statement about how he had "heard the call of duty" and had been persuaded, despite his reservations, to seek the office of president solely for "the good of the country." There was much applause and hand-shaking and the sound of camera shutters clicking filled the air like a horde of crickets in heat. The governor even deigned to field a few questions.

"Governor, what are your plans for rejuvenating the nation's economy?"

"I believe that this here country's still got what it takes to be the leader of the global economy. American enterprise is still the greatest in the world and I'll stand by that statement."

"Governor, what will you do to curtail the epidemic of drugs and violence in our cities?"

"Let me go on the record by saying that I believe the future of our country rests with its young people. And the youth of America are being devastated by this plague of drugs. It's time to get tough on criminals and put them behind bars where they belong."

"Governor, are you prepared to take a position on a national health care program?"

"Well, as you know, I've always believed that everyone is entitled to the finest medical care they can afford. And I'll be studying that issue very carefully."

All in all, the governor handled himself well; Scoop could tell that Reginald and Bret were impressed. There were no serious gaffes and the crowd of Texans seemed to be genuinely enthusiastic over the prospect of their man running for national office. And it made the national evening news, neatly edited into a four-second sound byte and slipped between an advertisement for underarm deodorant and a story about a woman who had grown a rutabaga in the shape of Lyndon Johnson.

The campaign was underway.

3/ October – January

It began like this:

My fellow Americans, I come before you today during troubled times. Even as I speak, our country stands at a crossroads. On one side lies prosperity, on the other lies failure. On one side lies victory, on the other lies defeat. On one side lies hope, on the other lies despair. And it is our decision, our choice as free Americans, which way to turn. We can choose the path of fear, the path of trepidation and cowardice, and let the fast pace of modern times speed by us. Or we can choose the path of courage, the path of truth and righteousness, and boldly step forward into the future. My friends, I am here today to tell you I believe we should choose the second path. And I believe I know the way.

It had been constructed slowly, with much care and effort. The product of endless meetings and numerous drafts, it had been pieced together, word by word, sentence by sentence, over half-filled cups of lukewarm coffee and ashtrays overflowing with cigarette butts. It had been scrawled on cocktail napkins in dimly lit bars and etched into the margins of bright yellow legal pads. It had been so frequently revised—critiqued and edited and re-written again—that no one could rightly claim exclusive authorship of even a single sentence. It was, in fact, the governor's calling card, his introduction to the vast number of American voters who had never heard of him before, and he carried it with him from town to town and from hotel to hotel along the campaign trail. To the members of his staff, it was know simply as The Speech.

And, of course, it was utter nonsense. Where precisely were these crossroads that politicians always seemed to be insisting America was standing at? Scoop wondered. To his thinking, the country was no more at a turning point than it usually was during an election campaign; the only significant choice the American people had to make was about which idiot to send to the White House next. According to The Speech, of course, the nation was standing between the paths of victory and defeat and the governor was wisely choosing the former. A very brave decision, thought Scoop. Who the hell would choose otherwise? He tried to imagine what the response of the crowd might be if the governor just once stood up and said, "We have a choice between hope and despair and I choose despair. Vote for me."

I am running for president, not as a conservative or as a liberal, not as a spokesman for some special interest group, not as a representative of any narrow segment of the population, but as a simple man who cares about the American people—all the American people. I care about the poor and the middle-class. I care about the black and the white. I care about the workers and the business people. I care about the farmers and the urban dwellers. I care about children and I care about the elderly.

Right, thought Scoop. Let's see, did we leave anyone out? Oh yeah, the handicapped. You care about the handicapped too, Governor. Make that the physically challenged. No, the differently abled. And puppy dogs. You care about puppy dogs, too. You care about all the poor black-and-white working-class rural- and urban-dwelling differently-abled puppy dogs. And their elderly grandmothers.

Why am I running for president? I'm glad you asked that question. I'm running because I want to make America a better place for us and our children and our children's children. I believe that all Americans have the right to equal opportunity, to live and work in freedom. I believe all children have the right to a good education. I believe that a strong America is a safe America. I believe criminals should be put in jail where they belong. I believe in the sanctity of the family. And I believe that the future of our country rests with its young people.

Jeez, Governor, thought Scoop, you're really going out on a limb there. I mean, you're in favor of families *and* education *and* putting criminals in jail? Wow, that's really going to send some shockwaves through the old American political scene. Yes sir, that's really going to turn some heads. If you don't watch out, you're going to get a reputation as some sort of radical. I'll bet none of the other candidates have the guts to take a stand on the tough issues like that. No sir, no one but you, Governor. Oh, but Governor, I don't suppose you'd care to kick a few specifics our way, would you? Say, give us a hint about what precisely you'd do regarding education or putting criminals in jail? Maybe fill us in on an actual program or policy you'd like to implement? No? No, I didn't think so.

Today, America stands poised on the brink of the future. It is a time of new beginnings, of a recommitment to the American dream. It is a time to rekindle the torch of freedom and pass it on to the next generation. It is a time for new leadership with new ideas. It is a time to put democracy back in the hands of true Americans everywhere. It is a time to celebrate the glory of a strong America, one nation under God, with liberty and justice for all. It is the dawning of a new age for America. Thank you and God bless.

Scoop was particularly fond of the part about being "poised on the brink of the future," a melodramatic expression which, as far as he could fathom, was completely meaningless. Strictly speaking, wasn't everything always poised on the brink of the future—be it today or five minutes from now or three weeks ago last Thursday? Not that anything else in The Speech made any more sense. With its mixture of traditionalism and so-called "new ideas," The Speech bordered on downright schizophrenic. Still, it was precisely the sort of bombastic, self-important drivel the voters seemed to thrive on. The audiences to whom the governor delivered The Speech listened with such rapt attention and responded with such enthusiastic applause that Scoop couldn't help but marvel at their sheer gullibility. He had seen it a thousand times before in a hundred other political campaigns, but the capacity of the American people to swallow such large and unadulterated doses of raw horseshit never ceased to amaze him.

And swallow they did, swallowed it whole, not in spite of the fact that The Speech really didn't say anything, but precisely *because* it didn't say anything. With its tired rhetoric and vague promises of a better tomorrow, it was wholly unobjectionable; there wasn't a single word in it to which any reasonable person could take exception. And when the governor spoke of patriotism, each listener formed his own idea of what that meant. And when the governor made reference to some wholly undefined future policies, each listener would mentally fill in the details herself. So that, when the governor finished speaking, each person felt that he or she understood perfectly what had been said and knew that the governor had indeed spoken the truth.

And that, of course, was precisely what The Speech had been designed to do. It was a do-it-yourself manifesto, a fill-in-the-blanks platform, a great Rorschach blot of a speech, full of sound and fury, as the poet would have it, and certainly signifying not a goddamn thing.

Contributions to the governor's campaign poured in.

By this point, the campaign was proceeding at a furious pace. The governor and his staff arose every morning by 5:30 and met to review the day's agenda. The governor then gave radio interviews over the telephone to as many local stations as he could until 7:30. The rest of the day was spent at campaign events, delivering The Speech and rubbing elbows with the populace at shopping malls, sporting events, plant cafeterias, parking lots, anywhere the governor could be assured of drawing a crowd. Evenings were reserved for fund-raising dinners and, frequently, private meetings with potentially large contributors. Then the governor and the whole staff would grab their bags and race to the nearest airport to catch the red-eye flight to whatever their next destination happened to be. The next morning by 5:30 everyone was awake and the whole thing started up again. It was an exhausting schedule.

"Governor, are you in favor of extending welfare benefits for the many people who are out of work in this country?"

"Let me say this and I mean it from the bottom of my heart. Every American who is capable of holding down a job should have the right to do so. I'll stand by that statement to the end. Now unfortunately there are some folks out there who are perfectly capable of working but would rather stay on welfare. These people are a drain on the economy and are living off the taxpayers' money. What we need to do is give jobs to the people who want to work, get the others off the taxpayers' backs, and provide a safety net for the truly needy."

At an elementary school in Illinois, the governor spoke about the importance of education and how "the future of our country rests with its young people." A boy from the fourth grade asked the governor why he was running for president. The governor responded that he wanted to make America a better place for the boy and the boy's children.

"Yeah," said the boy, "but why are you *really* running for president?"

On one side lies prosperity, on the other failure. On one side lies victory, on the other defeat. On one side lies hope...

In a hotel room in Denver, the governor excused himself from a meeting with a private contributor. He cornered Reginald in the hallway.

"This guy Remnick is loaded with dough," he said. "But he keeps dropping hints that he wants something in return."

"Like what specifically?"

"Like an ambassadorship. To China."

"So what's the problem?"

"We already told that chump Watney in New York I'd make him ambassador to China."

"So give it to both of them," said Reginald. "What's the difference? Since you have no intention of winning, you'll never actually have to make good on your promise to either of them."

"Oh, yeah," said the governor. "I hadn't thought of that."

At a campaign stop in Michigan: "Governor, do you support the president's foreign aid program or do you believe we should be keeping more money in this country to spend on domestic programs?"

"I believe the United States is the greatest nation on the face of the earth and, as such, we can't allow ourselves to be tempted into an isolationist foreign policy. At the same time, we have plenty of uses for our tax dollars in this country without shipping them overseas. So in answer to your question, yes, I do."

As the campaign wore on, the governor seemed to become more and more adept at fielding the questions of reporters. He preferred dealing with the reporters from smaller newspapers and radio stations; they were usually thrilled to be interviewing an honest-to-God presidential candidate and so, careful not to offend him, they didn't ask particularly probing questions nor challenge much that the governor said, basically allowing him to use the interview as an unpaid commercial. But even reporters from larger news agencies weren't much more difficult to handle. Most of them asked the same standard questions—it was rare for a reporter to actually come up with a new angle—and the governor had a scripted reply for each topic. Sometimes the reply didn't exactly match the question, but the reporters never seemed to take him to task for that. Most of them seemed more concerned with finding a juicy quote than with genuinely exploring the issues. Occasionally, when the governor wanted the chance to address a particular topic, his staff would plant someone in the audience to ask the appropriate question. On such occasions, the governor's answers fit the questions much more neatly.

...not as a representative of any narrow segment of the population, but as a simple man who cares about the American people—all the American people. I care about the poor and the middle-class. I care about the black and the white...

On a midnight flight from New York to Florida, the governor looked up from a half-eaten ham sandwich, his eyes bleary from lack of sleep.

"Where do I stand on abortion?" he asked.

Reginald considered the question. "Depends who asks. Best not to take too strong a stance on either side of the issue. We don't want to alienate any potential contributors. But I think it's safe to say if you're asked the question on one of the coasts, you should probably stress the rights of women. If you're asked the question in the South or the Midwest, on the other hand, it might be better to talk about the sanctity of life and how much you love children, that sort of thing. But as I said, best not to come down too heavily either way."

"Not too heavily," Bret concurred.

"Uh-huh," said the governor.

Reginald loosened his tie and looked out the window of the 747. He sat staring into the utter blackness as if considering the question further.

"Also," he said finally, "if the question is asked by a woman, you might want to say something a bit self-effacing."

"A bit self-deprecating," added Bret.

"Huh? What do you mean?"

"You know," said Reginald, "something like 'As a man, I can never fully understand the trauma a woman goes through when she has an abortion.' Women love when a male politician acts deferential. Makes them feel important. You understand what I mean?"

"Yeah," said the governor. "I s'pose so."

At a shopping mall in Iowa, the governor spoke about the decreasing value of the dollar and about how "all Americans have the right to equal opportunity." At a chemical plant in New Hampshire, he spoke about the plight of the working man and how "American enterprise is still the greatest in the world." At a playground in California, he spoke about the importance of the American family and had himself photographed, surrounded by children.

"Governor, there's been a great deal of controversy lately about our imbalance of trade with other nations. Do you believe that America should adopt protectionist trade practices in order to correct this imbalance?"

"Well now, I've always believed that America comes first and I'm willing to do whatever it takes to keep our nation number one. But that doesn't mean banning all imports. No sir, that's just asking for trouble. You can't hog-tie a bronco and still expect it to give you a good ride. Of course, other countries have to learn that America is going to look out for its own best interest. I believe in trade that's free and open, but most of all fair."

And still the money poured in, both from individual contributions and from large corporate PACs—the Committee to Rejuvenate American Business, the Committee to Promote Nuclear Energy, the Committee to Repeal Auto Emission Standards, the Committee to Even Further Deregulate the Banking Industry, ad infinitum. To each of them the governor gave his warmest thanks and his most heartfelt assurances that he would champion their cause above all others once elected to the White House.

I believe that a strong America is a safe America. I believe that criminals should be put in jail where they belong. I believe in the sanctity of the family...

In New York City, the governor spoke about the importance of civil rights and how "all Americans have the right to equal opportunity." In Jackson, Mississippi, he spoke about his opposition to racial quotas and how "all Americans have the right to equal opportunity."

In Atlanta, he flipped a coin before stepping to the podium.

By this point the governor had already staffed a number of Presidential commissions several times over. There was to be a commission to investigate the harms of pornography and a commission to analyze the dangers of censorship, a commission to explore alternative forms of energy and a commission to find new ways to support the oil industry, a commission to study hunger in America and a commission to make recommendations on ways to further cut federal spending on social programs. And, of course, appointments to any or all of these commissions were freely given in exchange for generous contributions.

But even those who didn't request a Presidential appointment expected *something* in exchange for their support. This is not to suggest that they intended to bribe the candidate; such an act would have been blatantly unethical, not to mention potentially punishable by law. No, they merely hoped to retain the candidate's attentiveness once he took office, to have a certain ease of access to which the average constituent could not lay claim. If they found themselves in trouble with, say, the Justice Department or the Internal Revenue Service, for example, they expected to be able to cut through the layers of governmental red tape and speak directly to the official involved in their case, the one most capable of aiding their cause. Surely there was nothing wrong with that. It was the American way, a mere greasing of the wheels, a circumvention of the cumbersome bureaucratic channels to which, regrettably, the average citizen (who, either through a lack of money or foresight or both, had somehow failed to make the requisite $1000 maximum personal contribution to the right candidate) could not avail himself. And surely that could not be misconstrued as bribery. It was simply a part of the system, a part which neither the governor nor his staff felt any compunction about exploiting. So the governor promised his contributors that they would have access to the top officials at the Department of Commerce, would be privy to the most confidential musings of the chairman of the Federal Reserve Board, would sit at the table of the Attorney General himself every morning for breakfast if they so desired. All this for a mere thousand dollars.

"Governor, what is your position on a woman's reproductive rights?"

The governor thought quickly. Where was he again? Montana? No, that was yesterday. Tennessee? No, not until next week. He tried to detect some discernible accent in the voice of his questioner, a thirty-ish woman in a red dress.

"Let me say this," he responded. "Abortion is a very serious matter and should not simply be used as a means of birth control. I believe that society has a responsibility to balance the rights of women and the rights of children. I believe that women must exercise control over their own bodies, but I also believe in the sanctity of the family.

"Of course," he added, "as a man I can never fully understand the trauma a woman goes through when she has an abortion."

The woman smiled.

One day the governor found himself riding a snowplow in Vermont after a blizzard had dumped eight inches of snow on Burlington. Cameras clicked and whirred. The next day he was touring a factory in Arizona that manufactured those little forks you stick in the ends of a cob of corn so you can eat it without burning your fingers. The governor smiled and waved. He went bowling with a bunch of blue-collar workers in Florida and shook hands with the crew that worked the closing shift at a McDonald's in the state of Washington. He went shopping for socks at a K-Mart in Dayton, Ohio and had bologna sandwiches with Local 237 of the United Electrical Workers in Richfield, Utah.

Today, America stands poised on the brink of the future. It is a time of new beginnings, of a recommitment to the American dream...

The states all began to blend together now, the hundred generic hotel rooms becoming indistinguishable. The first question that came to Scoop every morning when he awoke was *Where the hell am I?* He would check the cover of the phone book in the top drawer of the night table next to the bed. He would also call the weather service before getting dressed, so that he knew whether to expect temperatures in the seventies or ten below zero. The meals he ate rarely gave a hint of his location as he usually kept to the same diet wherever he went—eggs, hamburgers, sandwiches—and avoided the regional delicacies. Let the governor eat bagels at a breakfast with Jewish voters in New York, pork rinds and grits in the South, tacos and enchiladas in New Mexico. Scoop had been on enough national campaigns and knew better than to commit such an act of intestinal suicide. He appreciated the fact that fried clams at the Howard Johnson's in Fort Worth, Texas tasted exactly like fried clams at the Howard Johnson's in Bismarck, North Dakota. Scrambled eggs and Big Macs tasted the same everywhere and that was fine with him.

The crowds of people along the campaign trail blended together as well, the thousands of individual faces melded into a mask of anonymity, the face of the composite voter. The voter who was working and the voter who was unemployed, the voter who wanted less crime in the streets and the voter who wanted more teachers in the classroom, the voter worried about nuclear proliferation and the voter worried about where his next meal was coming from. The black auto worker from Detroit and the white college student from New England, the man wearing a hardhat at a factory on the East Coast and the woman with the picket sign on the West Coast, the elderly woman living on Social Security in the city and the five-year-old boy in overalls on the Iowa farm.

No one on the campaign actually had the time to get to know any of these people, not really know them. No one had the time to see them as individuals or to really understand what their concerns were. The campaign simply moved too fast; the best one could manage was to glimpse their faces as they sped by. Certainly the governor didn't have the time—or the inclination—to actually listen, only to pretend to listen and to nod with feigned commiseration. And to smile and shake their hands and then to move on because there were so many other hands still left to shake.

...one nation, under God, with liberty and justice for all. It is the dawning of a new age for America. Thank you and God bless.

On a night flight to New Hampshire, Scoop leaned back in his seat, utterly spent. He had a pounding headache which was only exacerbated by the barely discernible whine that seemed to be emanating from the cabin's pressurization system. He tore open a package of salted almonds and tossed a few in his mouth, then washed them down with a sip of Dewar's. It would have to do for tonight's dinner. Scoop didn't particularly mind; he was far more interested in sleep than food at the moment.

I'm not moving from this seat until I've slept a few hours, he thought. Even if the goddamn plane crashes, I'm not budging.

"Not bad," said Bret from the seat to his left. He had a confusion of papers spread out on top of the briefcase in his lap and was punching numbers into a handheld calculator.

"Good news?" asked Scoop, although at the moment he was barely interested.

"Excellent," said Bret. "So far we've raised seven and a half million dollars. Lower than expected, but still leaving us a generous profit after expenses. Better yet, we've managed to do it without significantly increasing the governor's name recognition. According to yesterday's NBC poll, the vast majority of Americans still haven't the slightest idea who Thurmond Stonewall is or what he stands for. So even though our coffers are full, the country still doesn't see the governor as a serious candidate."

Bret reached up to turn off the light above his seat, then settled back with a sigh. The cabin seemed almost peaceful now in the half light, the only sounds being the low whistle of air escaping from the overhead fans and, from somewhere behind them, the governor's snoring.

"Scoop?"

"Yeah?"

"What's your prediction? How do you think we'll do in the Iowa precinct caucuses?"

Scoop took another sip of scotch. "To put it bluntly, I think we're gonna get our asses kicked."

In the dim light, Scoop could see an impish, almost childlike smile spreading across Bret's face.

Yes," said Bret. "I do believe you're right."

4/ Iowa, February 8th

The other Democratic candidates running for President were a diverse bunch. Polls indicated that the two favorites were Ed Mondukis and Lloyd Yeager. Senator Mondukis was the worst stereotype of the traditional New Deal Democrat who seemed to believe that any problem could be solved provided enough money was thrown at it. Mondukis was already lining up the support of many of the country's largest labor unions and had the backing of the liberal faction of the Democratic Party. Yeager, on the other hand, was the conservative governor of Ohio and a genuine war hero, having received the Congressional Medal of Honor after serving two tours of duty as a colonel in Korea. Many in the party believed Yeager to be the most electable Democrat, primarily because he looked and sounded exactly like a Republican.

The field was filled out by players whose prospects were somewhat more doubtful. For example, according to most political pundits, 75-year-old Senator Hubert Stevenson, the most liberal of the candidates, couldn't even have gotten himself elected to clean the White House men's room. But then that had never stopped him from running before. In fact, Stevenson had been running for President every four years for as long as anyone could remember and had never come close to capturing the party's nomination. He never lost hope, though, just as he never seemed to age, a phenomenon which prompted some members of the press to dub him "the Dick Clark of American politics" and others to speculate about whether he had a portrait locked away in his attic that was growing more and more decrepit with each new campaign. Then there was industrial tycoon Howard Ruff—or, as the press rather facetiously referred to him, "The Howard." Ruff was running on a strong pro-business platform and with his speeches full of Japan-bashing and "America First" rhetoric and his radical proposal to completely eliminate the capital gains tax, he was actually attracting more Republicans than Democrats to his campaign.

Actor Warren MacClaine had also thrown his hat into the ring. A star of numerous grade-B action flicks, he was best known in the role of tough cop Big Jim McShaw in a series of movies with titles like "Brute Force" and "Blood Shot." MacClaine had retired from acting to become mayor of Beverly Hills and was now running for President on a "tough on crime" platform. MacClaine's people had made the dubious decision to have his campaign run out of a West Coast public relations firm with a background in movie publicity, rather than one stationed in New York or Washington with more experience in political advertising. The result was a campaign poster that featured a photograph of MacClaine in his Big Jim tough-guy pose, Magnum .357 drawn and cocked, while the slogan below paraphrased one of the most famous lines from his films: "Go Ahead. Make Me President."

Rounding out the field was the Reverend Al Washington, the only black candidate. Washington had built a national reputation by being a fiery spokesman for minority rights, but now that he was running for president he feared that his rhetoric might alienate white voters. As a result, he was soft-pedaling his racial message and trying to appeal more to the mainstream. Unfortunately, this shift also served to make him rather bland and he was now in danger of becoming even whiter than Michael Jackson.

And, of course, there was Thurmond Stonewall.

Everything had been going as anticipated for the Stonewall campaign, which is to say it was facing almost certain defeat. The plan was for the governor to enroll in all of the early primaries. He would then spend as little money as possible and garner as few votes as possible in each state. Sometime after Super Tuesday, with the campaign going nowhere and the response of the voters embarrassingly tepid, the political pundits would begin to declare Stonewall dead as a candidate. And eventually, allowing just enough time to make it look as if the decision were a reluctant one, the governor would throw his support and his meager collection of electoral votes to one of the other candidates and sadly, regretfully, withdraw from the race with the honorable justification that it was, without doubt, "in the best interest of the Democratic Party." All very noble and, of course, quite profitable.

The governor was almost looking forward to his concession speech. He imagined himself standing before the television cameras, his collar slightly askew in a rugged manner and his brow beaded with sweat from the rigors of the campaign trail. And the crowd of supporters—or however many his staff could scrape together, at any rate—would be standing before him, chanting his name and begging him not to give up the fight. But he would only look straight ahead, with strength and determination in his eyes, and make the announcement they were all dreading they would hear. Yes, he would sacrifice his own political interests for the good of the party and he would do so gracefully, scolding his loyal supporters to be of good cheer in this most trying of times and calling for a new air of unity and mutual respect among his former rivals for the nomination, that they resist the temptations of mud-slinging and back-stabbing and remember that they were all fellow foot-soldiers in the greater war, the contest against the Republicans that would be decided in the general election. And with great dignity he would hold back the tears and force a smile as he posed beside his wife. And the next day he might actually find himself on the front page of daily newspapers across the country, striking that heroic pose. And for that one moment, the governor's name would be on the lips of every American, his face on every television screen, as all applauded his act of noble good will. And the country would know, if only for a brief instant in its long history, what a man like Thurmond Stonewall was truly made of.

"Shit."

"What?" said the governor, shaking himself from his reverie.

"I don't fucking believe this," said Scoop. "Reg, get in here!"

They were sitting in a suite of hotel rooms in Des Moines, the closest they had to a campaign headquarters in Iowa. The rooms were a shambles of unmade beds and half-unpacked suitcases and, in the midst of all the clutter, Scoop had pulled a chair and a bottle of Dewar's up to the television in order to monitor the early returns from the state's precinct caucuses. Throughout the evening the screen had been filled with numbers and bar graphs and other colorful computer graphics, while the network anchors exuded an air of self-importance and the kind of excitement that television usually reserved for game shows and the recitation of winning lottery numbers.

When the early returns had begun trickling in, the results were pretty much what had been expected. Earl Jeeter and the Worthington brothers, convinced that there would be no surprises, had long since abandoned their vigil in front of the television set and had wandered into the adjoining room while the governor, who hadn't been paying all that much attention in the first place, had proceeded to sack out on the bed with a week-old copy of *Sports Illustrated*. But now, as the evening grew late and returns were coming in from more and more precincts, the voting was beginning to show an unexpected trend.

"What is it?" asked Reginald as he strode into the room, his hair slightly ruffled and a glass of Perrier in his hand.

"Trouble," said Scoop. "Take a look."

Reginald glanced at the television, where the latest projections were being flashed on-screen. According to the results of exit polls, Ed Mondukis and Lloyd Yeager were running neck-in-neck for first place— followed, just behind, by one Governor Thurmond Stonewall. Reginald smiled.

"Very amusing. Of course, nothing to panic about. I'm sure it's just a fluke. It will straighten itself out once the returns are in from all the precincts. Mark my words."

But when the early editions hit the stands the following morning, Mondukis was the clear winner with a projected 35%, followed by Yeager with 30% and, coming in third, Stonewall with 12%. The other four candidates split the remaining votes fairly evenly.

That morning, throughout the state of Iowa, an important rite was being enacted—the time-honored morning-after campaign ritual known as spin control, a curious process in which each candidate meets with his staff and advisors to discuss the results of the prior evening's election and, thereupon, frantically attempts to put the best possible face on the situation. In no time at all, the national media would be filled with claims of victory from each candidate. It made no difference if he received thirty votes or thirty thousand, whether he received an absolute majority or was shut-out at the polls. Each campaign would interpret the results in its own fashion, using whatever type of reasoning was necessary, however convoluted and contrary to common sense it might seem, in order to give the appearance that its man had indeed won.

That morning in Reginald's hotel room, the staff of the Stonewall campaign attended a meeting as well, but the focus was somewhat different.

"How could this have happened?" Jeeter asked no one in particular, his voice quivering nervously. "We barely even campaigned in Iowa! We didn't even have a headquarters!"

"Okay, we can handle this," said Reginald, pouring himself a cup of coffee with extra cream and an embarrassing amount of sugar. "Let's just calm down and take it one step at a time."

"One step at a time," said Bret.

"Look here, boy," said the governor. "I may not know much about these here primaries, but where I come from twelve percent ain't exactly a landslide. So what's all the goddamn fuss about?"

"Because it's not bad enough!" said Jeeter.

"Beg pardon?" said the governor.

"What Earl's saying is we did better than anyone expected us to," explained Reginald. "We barely campaigned in the state, but we still picked up twelve percent. The press is going to interpret that as a victory."

"So even though we lost, we won," said Bret.

"Now *why* we picked up twelve percent is another matter entirely," continued Reginald. "Scoop?"

"Based on what people said in exit polls, most voters still don't have a clear idea who the governor is or what he stands for," said Scoop. "Unfortunately, the voters *do* know who the *other* candidates are and they don't like it. I think most of the ballots that were cast for the governor were protest votes. The other candidates were simply perceived as being such complete dolts that the governor starting looking good by comparison. In this case it turns out it was better the devil you *don't* know than the one you do."

"Well then, that ain't all bad, is it?" asked the governor, "I mean, if we did okay in Iowa, won't more folks start making donations to the campaign?"

"True enough," said Reginald, "but it's all a matter of balance. The better we do in the state elections, the longer we'll be expected to stay in the race. And the longer we stay in the race, the more money we have to spend in order to make it look good. So even though we'll be taking more money in, we'll also have to put more money out. Already some of the more astute members of the press have noticed that we seem to be running a 'shoestring' campaign."

"That's another consideration," added Bret. "The better we seem to be doing, the more press attention we'll be attracting. And we don't want anyone examining the campaign too closely."

"That's right, I hadn't even thought of that." Earl bit his lip and wiped beads of sweat from his oversized forehead with a handkerchief. "If we're not careful, we could wind up all over the headlines!"

"Calm down, Earl," said Scoop. "This campaign couldn't cop a headline if the governor gave birth. So let's not start panicking."

"Scoop is right," said Reginald. "We can handle this. We just have to take steps to assure that we nip this thing in the bud, as it were. We need to put an end to the governor's newfound popularity with the voters as rapidly as possible."

The governor squinted in confusion. "What do you mean, put an end to it?"

Reginald leaned back in his chair and allowed a mischievous smile to play on his lips. "To put it simply, we sabotage the campaign."

"Sabotage?" asked the governor. "How?"

"Any number of ways," Scoop interjected. "A candidate's popularity is a damn fragile thing. One false move in any of a thousand different directions and he's stepping in dog shit. Remember Muskie in '72? He was way out in front of all the other candidates. Then the Manchester Union Leader starts trashing his wife on the editorial page and he's seen on national TV with tears in his eyes. Voters ran from him in droves. He was too emotional. In '88, Bernard Shaw fires a question at Dukakis about what he'd do if his wife were raped. Dukakis answered without batting an eyelash. People dumped *him* in a hurry, too. He was too *un*emotional." Scoop took a long gulp of black coffee. "As I said, one false move."

"So what do you suggest in this case?" asked Reginald. "What do you think would be most effective?"

"I ain't crying," said the governor. "I ain't crying on national TV, no how. I don't care what anyone says."

"I'm sure that won't be necessary, Governor," Reginald assured him.

Scoop grabbed a yellow legal pad and began scribbling notes. "Tell me, Governor, are there any skeletons in your closet? Anything you haven't told us about?"

The governor sat up straight and jutted his chin out as if he were posing for a postage stamp. "No sir, there sure ain't. I've never done anything I'm ashamed of. Not a single thing. My record is spotless."

Scoop stopped writing and looked up quizzically over the top of the legal pad. "C'mon, Governor, get real. You've been in politics for sixteen years. Before that you were a lawyer, for Christ's sake. And you expect us to believe you don't have any dirty laundry? Bullshit."

The governor's face flushed with emotion. "I don't have to sit here and listen to this. Not from the people in my own campaign, hell no. What are you calling me, boy? You calling me a liar?"

"Governor," said Reginald, "I'm sure Scoop didn't mean any—"

"Come on, Governor," Scoop continued, seemingly oblivious to the emotional response his questioning had provoked. "Think back. Somewhere back there, there must be something—some small, insignificant event—that wasn't completely on the up-and-up. Something that wasn't one-hundred percent kosher. Isn't there? Isn't there something? Think, Governor. Anything at all."

The governor grew quiet for a moment and seemed to study the white Styrofoam coffee cup in his hand. He rolled the cup slowly back and forth between his palms and made a series of indentations in the soft Styrofoam with his thumbnail.

"Well, there is one thing," he said finally, in a voice quieter than anyone would have thought him capable.

"Tell us," said Scoop.

"It was years ago."

"No matter."

"I mean really, years ago. I was just a boy, for God's sake. It was a, a…what do you call it?…a youthful indiscretion, that's what it was. Why, I was no older than a—"

"I don't care if it was pre-natal," said Scoop. "Tell us, already."

"Well, it's just that some folks are naturally good at it and some aren't is all. Don't have anything to do with how smart you are, really. Some folks just find it easier than others. For me, it's always been kind of an ordeal."

"Governor, *what* are you talking about?"

"I'm talking about tests, that's all. Taking tests. I mean, it ain't like I didn't know the material or anything. Knew it better than most, far as I'm concerned. Made a damn good lawyer, do say so myself. Just somehow putting it all down on paper got me fouled up. I remember all through college, the mid-terms, the finals…"

"You cheated on your college finals?" asked Scoop, groping for meaning. "Is that what you're driving at?"

"Well, it ain't goddamn fair," said the governor. "I mean, I've wanted to be a lawyer since I was knee-high to a heifer. And it all comes down to one test. One goddamn test. I mean, I ask you. Is that fair?"

Scoop's eyes grew wide as the realization sank in. "You mean the *bar*?"

"Hell, it ain't like I didn't do the work," continued the governor. "I did the damn work. I worked just as hard as anyone else. Harder than most. I—"

"The state bar exam?" repeated Scoop. "Are you saying you cheated on the state bar exam?"

"Well for God's sake, after doing all that work, to have it all come down to one goddamn test. It ain't fair. It just…" The governor's voice trailed off as he seemed to deplete his supply of both words and emotions simultaneously. "…ain't fair…"

"You cheated on your bar exam," repeated Scoop. "That *is* what you're saying, isn't it? You cheated on your bar exam."

The governor flinched as if stung by a hornet. "Well for God's sake, a lot of folks have done worse. Ain't like I killed someone or anything. It ain't *that* bad."

"Bad?" said Scoop, "*Bad*?! It's great! It's fantastic! It's absolutely perfect! You cheated on your bar exam!"

"Jesus, keep it down, will you?" The governor glanced nervously around the room, as if there might be someone sitting there who hadn't already heard the news, "You don't have to go telling everyone."

"But that's *exactly* what we're going to do," said Scoop. "That's exactly it." Scoop bolted from his chair, threw open the window and stuck his head out. "Hey, everybody! Hey! Presidential candidate Thurmond Stonewall cheated on his state bar exam!"

"Jesus fucking Christ," said the governor, "will you tell that asshole to get back in here?"

"That's enough, Scoop," said Reginald.

Scoop closed the window and flopped back into his chair, clearly enjoying the governor's discomfort.

"Goddamn son of a…," muttered the governor.

"Okay," Reginald said to Scoop, "now that we've got this, what do we do with it?"

Scoop thought for a moment. "We're going to have to be careful how we leak this. We want to make sure that no one will be able to trace it back to the governor's own campaign. Also, we don't want it buried on the bottom of page seventeen in the papers. I don't suppose there's any way to prove that you cheated after all this time, is there, Governor?"

The governor glared at Scoop. "No," he said flatly.

"Uh-huh. So what we've really got here is a hot rumor, nothing more. In order to get the most bang for the buck, I say we plant it in the governor's home state. What's the biggest daily paper in Texas?"

The governor was clearly reluctant to cooperate. "Don't know," he said shortly. "Houston Journal, I s'pose."

"The Houston Journal it is then," said Scoop. "No way they can ignore a story like this, not when it's about their own governor. My guess is they run it on page one. Then we just wait for the national media to pick up on it."

"Good," said Reginald, "it's set then. Take care of it, Scoop. In the meantime, the rest of us are going to have to start doing some serious campaigning in New Hampshire to make it look good."

And campaign they did. Operating out of a storefront headquarters in Manchester, the Stonewall staff worked as vigorously for their candidate as any one of the other staffs did for theirs—handing out leaflets, ringing doorbells, phoning registered Democrats throughout the state and asking for their support. And the governor was everywhere— shaking hands, delivering The Speech, rubbing elbows with the voters. The days were cold and overcast and a harsh wind was blowing down from Canada, but the excitement of the upcoming primary seemed to generate its own frenetic heat.

Meanwhile, Scoop kept a careful eye on The Houston Journal. But after one day, two days, three days, there was nothing.

"I don't understand it," Scoop said one night at campaign headquarters. They were sitting amongst a disarray of campaign posters and half-empty pizza boxes, discussing the past day's events and planning strategy for the next. Scoop had loosened his collar and rolled up his sleeves and he periodically swept his hand through his mass of tangled hair in exasperation. "I leaked the story days ago. The Journal should have *done* something by now. What the hell kind of newspaper are they running down there, for God's sake?"

Suddenly, the governor began to laugh, quietly at first, but then louder and with increasing mirth. "Well, goddamn" he managed between chuckles, "I should have known old Jim would stand by me. Yes sir, I guess I've still got me some true friends back there in the Lone Star state." His whole body convulsed with laughter and his face turned red as overripe fruit.

"What the hell are you talking about?" demanded Scoop. "Jim who?"

The governor regained control of himself and wiped the moisture from his eyes. "Why Jim McPierson, of course. Editor of The Houston Journal. I should have known he'd never publish a story like that about me, even if it was true."

"What are you saying? You *know* the editor of The Houston Journal?"

"'Course I know him," said the governor. "Don't be a goddamn fool. Why wouldn't I know him? I'm the governor, for Christ's sake. Good old Jim has been a big supporter of mine for years. Why I remember when him and me was back in college together. Used to go out drinking every weekend. I remember this one time we went to this little strip joint outside of Sugarland. Seems there was this dancer there who—"

"Please, Governor, spare us," said Reginald. He shook his head slowly in exasperation. "Why didn't you tell us you were personal friends with the editor of the Houston newspaper?"

The governor smiled and shrugged. "No one asked me." And then to Scoop he added: "Gotcha!"

Scoop rolled his eyes. "Great. Just fucking great."

"Well, what do we do now?" asked Bret.

Scoop thought for a moment. "Okay, to hell with Texas," he

announced. "No more screwing around. This time we go straight for the national market. I'm leaking the story to The Daily American."

The Daily American was the country's largest selling daily newspaper. A slick national tabloid, it was evidently designed for readers with limited attention spans as none of its articles ever ran for more than a few paragraphs and it used so many colorful graphs and pie charts on its front page that it sometimes more closely resembled a comic book than a newspaper at first glance. It also ran frequent contests on its front page in an attempt to increase its circulation. Scoop didn't trust The Daily American; he couldn't bring himself to trust any newspaper whose lead story every morning was "You Can Win Our Star-Spangled Sweepstakes!" But as crass as Scoop found it, the American people evidently ate it up. The Daily American was a sensation and easily out-sold most local newspapers around the country. If Scoop wanted to make an impact on the average American voter, he decided The Daily American was the perfect target.

Two days later, he stormed into campaign headquarters, his face flushed with excitement and a copy of that day's edition of The Daily American thrust under his arm.

"What happened?" asked Reginald. "Did they run it?"

"Oh, they ran it all right," said Scoop. "Front page. Banner headline. Can't miss it."

"Really? Let me see."

"Oh, you want to see? Sure, I'll let you see. Here, take a good hard look."

Scoop slapped the newspaper down in front of Reginald. And there it was, covering the front page, in bold headlines two inches high: BRITNEY AND K-FED TO RE-WED.

"What the...," said Reginald, confused.

"What's that you say? You want to know if there are any articles inside? Why there are *pages* of articles inside! Each one only four paragraphs long, but pages of articles nonetheless! There's an article about Britney's new album. There's an article about K-Fed's new album. There's an interview with the priest who's going to perform the ceremony, an interview with the caterer, an interview with the caterer's goddamn hair-stylist..."

"But what...?"

"What's that?" said Scoop. "You want to know if there are any photos inside? Oh, there are *lots* of photos inside! There's a photo of the wedding dress. There's a photo of Britney wearing the wedding dress. There's a photo of Britney *not* wearing the wedding dress. Yup, lots and lots of photos, all nicely interspersed with pages and pages of fucking four-paragraph-long articles!"

"But the governor," Reginald finally managed to interject. "What about the story on the governor?"

"Oh, *that* story. Is *that* the story you want to read about? Well, if you can manage to make your way through the eight pages of Britney and K-Fed stories, I believe you'll find...yes, here it is." Scoop flipped open the newspaper. There at the bottom of page seventeen was a tiny, one-paragraph article alleging that one of the presidential candidates may have cheated on his bar exam. The name of the candidate mentioned in the article was Thurston Stimwell.

"Who the hell is Thurston Stimwell?" said Reginald.

"Beats the fuck out of me," said Scoop. "Ask Britney."

"Okay," said Reginald, maintaining his composure, "we can handle this. Let's not get carried away. According to the latest polls, we haven't a chance of repeating our Iowa success in New Hampshire. So all we need do is raise the expectations of the press. Tell them we expect to do outstandingly in the primary. Then no matter how well we do, it will look like a defeat."

"Right," said Scoop, taking a deep breath. His face was starting to return to its normal color now. "That's good. Very good. Okay, how about this? We predict that we're going to get...say, twenty-five percent of the vote."

"Excellent," said Reginald. "The polls don't even put us at half that amount. That's perfect. Twenty-five percent it is."

But the New Hampshire primary is a singularly unpredictable event. It is where careers are made and hearts are broken, where images are formed and hopes are dashed. In the days leading up to the primary, it is all anyone talks about; the entire state becomes a marketplace of ideas, with politics the main currency. And when the day of the primary finally arrives, the people of New Hampshire carry themselves to the polls with an air of self-importance, knowing that the rest of the nation is watching them, knowing that for this one day out of every four years, they will have an impact on the future of the country that is by any method of measurement completely disproportionate to their state's size or population. And, as if to deliberately frustrate the predictions of the pundits and analysts, the voters of New Hampshire cast their ballots as they choose.

On that particular primary day, a majority of them chose Governor Lloyd Yeager of Ohio to be the Democratic presidential candidate. But just behind him was Governor Thurmond Stonewall of Texas. Governor Stonewall had received a full twenty-six percent of the vote.

5/ Super Tuesday, March 8th

"Crap," said Scoop.

"What?" asked Reginald.

"I just got off the phone with CNN. King wants an interview."

"*Larry* King?"

"No, *Irving* King. Of course Larry King! Who the hell else?"

Nerves were frayed and tensions were running high in the weeks following the New Hampshire primary. And not just in the Stonewall campaign—most of the candidates were finding significant stumbling blocks in their paths to the party's nomination, many having fared poorly in the Maryland, Georgia, Colorado, Utah and Idaho primaries. Hubert Stevenson, the aging liberal, had already ended his candidacy, having received less than ten percent of the vote in two consecutive primaries, thereby making him ineligible for further federal matching funds. Faced with near-empty campaign coffers and the prospect of competing in the expensive Super Tuesday primaries, Stevenson chose to withdraw from the race. But no one doubted that he would return four years hence, ripe and ready and full of vigor, to take another futile stab at the presidency at the age of 79.

Actor Warren MacClaine had also called it quits. His campaign had actually been doing better than many had predicted until he punched out an Associated Press reporter who had made the mistake of asking him why he didn't have an economic policy. Afterwards, MacClaine announced that he was retiring from politics altogether and returning to acting. He had already signed a contract to appear in a new film, this one entitled *Death Fist*.

Industrialist Howard Ruff had lost his federal matching funds as well, but that did little to discourage him since he was paying most of the campaign expenses out of his own pocket anyway. At the other end of the financial spectrum, Reverend Al Washington was somehow squeezing by with his grass-roots campaign, despite having done poorly in all the primaries so far. That left the two front-runners, Ed Mondukis and Lloyd Yeager, still in a virtual tie for first place. And of course, still solidly in third, Thurmond Stonewall.

The governor wasn't exactly winning any primaries. The problem was, he wasn't exactly losing them either. He was doing just well enough to exceed the rather modest predictions of the press, an unfortunate and unexpected turn of events which made it difficult for him to drop out of the race without it seeming suspicious. And now, with the Super Tuesday primaries approaching, the campaign was being forced to expend a large amount of capital in one lump sum in order to compete in eleven states simultaneously—not the most desirable course of action when one's ultimate goal is to turn a profit. Throughout the country, from Massachusetts to Mississippi and from Texas to Tennessee, the Stonewall campaign was frantically moving to establish and staff a slew of state campaign headquarters.

But it wasn't merely the outlay of funds which irked the staff of the Stonewall campaign. It was also the press attention that seemed to be increasing with each primary, attention that served to put everyone on edge. Even the governor, who up until then had seemed almost oblivious to the dangers of the Worthingtons' scheme, was beginning to express some worries.

"Goddamn," he said after capturing nearly 25% of the vote in Georgia, a state in which he hadn't even campaigned. "What the hell is going on? If we don't look out, we're going to start winning. And then what the hell do we do? What do we do if we start winning primaries?"

Reginald tried to reassure him. "Calm down, Governor. We are definitely not going to win any primaries. Nothing outside of Texas, at any rate. Believe me, my brother and I thoroughly researched your viability as a candidate and we wouldn't have picked you if we hadn't been absolutely convinced that you were a complete loser."

"You're just saying that to make me feel better," said the governor.

"No, I'm not," insisted Reginald. "It's true. Tell him, Bret."

"Absolutely true," said Bret. "A complete loser."

For once they were not packed into some disastrously cluttered room in a cheap, out-of-the-way motel. That's where most of the campaign staff meetings had been taking place over the past few weeks, as Bret insisted that they try to hold down expenses by accepting less than first-class accommodations. The governor and his staff had therefore found themselves staying at a sordid collection of ramshackle motor lodges and sleazy motels, some of which were more accustomed to renting rooms by the hour than by the week. More than once a meeting had been brought to a momentary halt by the distinct sounds of love-making, the moans of pleasure and creaking of bedsprings, emanating through paper-thin walls from the room next door.

But as Super Tuesday approached, and along with it the Texas primary, the governor had returned to the loving arms of his home state to bask in the affection of his constituents and to remind those of them who might have forgotten just how much he had done for them over the years. For the governor, it was like returning to a safe haven, a political oasis in the harsh desert of the campaign. For his staff, it was an opportunity to eat a home-cooked meal and to sleep, if only for a few nights, on sheets whose cleanliness they had no need to question.

And so they found themselves relaxing in the sumptuous living room of the governor's ranch, located on a wide expanse of land just outside of Austin, overlooking the Colorado River. The governor's wife had overseen the preparation and serving of an enormous Texan meal—steak, barbequed baby back ribs, black-eyed peas, homemade corn bread, and sweet potato pie—and had then retreated to one of the upstairs rooms, like the perfect political wife she had spent the last sixteen years learning to be, leaving the men to bask in the afterglow of excessive grease and carbohydrate consumption, to pick the final remnants of the meal from between their teeth, and to plot future campaign strategy.

"Super Tuesday," Reginald was saying. "Do you have any idea how expensive it's going to be to participate in the Super Tuesday primaries?"

"Very expensive," said Bret.

"*Very* expensive," said Reginald. He sank back into the plush sofa, his body seeming to relax but his face remaining incongruously pensive.

"If only there were a way...some way to end the campaign

quickly— quickly, definitively, and immediately—before having to compete in Super Tuesday."

"And without it looking suspicious," added Bret.

"Maybe there is," said Scoop. He was staring at the ice cubes in his drink so intently that at first it seemed he was addressing the glass. "What if the governor were to say something? Something that would totally discredit him in the eyes of the voters?"

"Like what?" asked the governor.

"It would have to be something pretty substantial," said Reginald. "I can't imagine a whole campaign going down the tubes over one misstatement."

Scoop pulled himself to his feet and began pacing back and forth across the living room. "But what if it were something that really pissed people off? Something totally outrageous. Like attacking a sacred cow."

"How about Social Security?" suggested Earl. "The governor could issue a statement saying he plans to slash Social Security. That would sure lose him some votes."

Scoop stopped pacing long enough to consider it. "True, that would be political suicide. But it wouldn't be quick enough. Given the federal deficit, some people might actually defend it as a legitimate point of view. No, I think we should look for something more shocking…more immediately offensive."

"Offensive?" Reginald furrowed his brow, "You mean like swearing into an open mike or something?"

"No, no, no," said Scoop, resuming his pacing. "That's far too easy to defend. Christ, *everybody* swears. A politician who didn't swear would probably come across as some kind of wimp. No, I'm talking about something that's completely inexcusable, completely unforgivable. Something the press will really kick the shit out of him for. Something so offensive to the average American that the idea of voting for Governor Stonewall would become utterly repellant." Scoop was pacing so rapidly now that the scotch was nearly sloshing over the sides of his glass.

"What the hell do you want me to do?" asked the governor. "Strangle a puppy on national TV? Bite the head off a goddamn chicken?"

All at once, Scoop came to a dead halt. "What if the governor were to say something racist?"

"Racist?" said Reginald.

"You mean like attacking affirmative action?" asked Earl. "Something like that?"

"No, not at all," said Scoop. "Lots of politicians criticize affirmative action. I'm talking about something a lot more flagrant. Something that couldn't be explained away as anything but out-and-out bigotry."

"You really think that'd work?" asked the governor.

Scoop shrugged. "Frankly, I don't know. Seems like it might be worth a shot. Reg, what do you think?"

"Hmm." Reginald seemed to consider the proposal for several moments before speaking. "I think it has potential. There's no doubt that it would cause serious damage to the campaign. But would it be enough to knock us out of the race completely?"

"It might, if the comment were made in a public-enough arena," said Scoop. "That way the governor can't possibly deny it after the fact. And it's got to sound as if it's coming straight from the governor himself, not being read off an index card or a prepared statement. We don't want anybody, even the governor's supporters, to be able to attribute this to anyone but the governor himself, completely and undeniably." Scoop made his way to the liquor cabinet to replenish his glass with Chivas Regal. It was far from his favorite scotch—too mellow and insubstantial for Scoop's taste, almost like the "light beer" equivalent of whiskey—but it was the only scotch the governor kept on hand.

"The way I see it is like this," Scoop continued after he had refilled his glass. "We get the governor into a high-profile situation. That's easy enough to do. Now at some point the governor appears to wander from his prepared text, maybe in response to a question or something like that. Of course, it'll only look like the governor's ad-libbing. We'll have the whole thing scripted out for you, Governor. Anyway, at that point the governor drops the bombshell. The press hears it and goes into attack mode. We sit back and do nothing for about twenty-four hours, enough time for the media to get the word out about what the governor said and to start declaring him unfit as a candidate. Then maybe we issue some sort of two-bit denial—you know, the governor's words are being taken out of context, he's being unfairly maligned by the press, the usual bullshit—some response that's obviously inadequate. This only turns up the pressure from the media— the governor's insensitive about the impact of his statement, he doesn't care about minorities, etc. By this point, the governor's standings in the polls have taken a nosedive. We're getting hecklers at his rallies, maybe even some demonstrators, and of course all of this is being reported by the press as well.

"Finally, the governor is forced to realize his campaign is doomed. He tucks his tail between his legs and withdraws from the race, the press says 'good riddance,' and a week later no one even remembers he was a candidate." Scoop flopped back down into his chair. "The end. Anyway, that's how I see it playing out."

There was a moment of silence as the others considered his words.

"All right," Reginald said finally. "Unless anyone has any better suggestions, I think we should implement it. The only question that remains, then, is where precisely do we drop this so-called 'bombshell?'"

"We've got the debate scheduled for later this week," suggested Earl. "How about there?"

"Of course!" said Reginald. "The debate! That's a perfect opportunity for the governor to appear to be speaking off-the-cuff. He'll be asked questions on any number of topics. Undoubtedly he'll have the opportunity to insert our little surprise into one of his answers."

"I like it," agreed Scoop. "Plus there are added advantages. The media will be covering the debate, so their response will be immediate. And the other candidates get to have a field day with it too. All right, then. The debate it is."

The governor had participated in a number of debates with the other Democratic candidates already. At the time he had been trailing in the polls and nobody was taking him seriously as a candidate. Dismissed by the press as an immediate also-ran and viewed by the other candidates as, at worst, a harmless annoyance, the governor had walked through the debates with fairly little effort. None of the other candidates had challenged him, none of the reporters had directed any of the tough questions to him. All attention had been focused on the two front-runners, Ed Mondukis and Lloyd Yeager, and their on-going efforts to attack each other's views and undermine each other's positions. As a result, Thurmond Stonewall had escaped completely unscathed. He had simply stuck to his script, mouthing the same vague generalities and delivering the same pre-written answers to questions. As of yet, nobody had tried to take him to the mat.

But the upcoming debate in Florida was expected to be a different story. The governor had achieved a certain amount of success at the polls and, even though nobody would have accused him of being a front-runner, the other candidates were beginning to view him a little more warily. The overall level of unpleasantness in the campaign had been on the rise as well, with the other candidates regularly accusing each other of a host of varied crimes and misdemeanors, ranging in nature and severity from draft evasion to drug use to marital infidelity. The press, of course, was decrying these campaign tactics and bemoaning the dearth of ideas and debate on the issues, even as they added more fuel to the fire by honoring each candidate's accusations and counter-accusations with headlines and front-page stories and consigning any serious discussion of the candidates' ideas to the fine print of the op-ed pages.

So the Stonewall staff was prepared for the Florida debate to be a test of fire and for their candidate, for the first time during the race, to be sucked into the whirlwind of accusations and innuendo that had become associated with the campaign. Of course, that prospect bothered no one. If some of the other candidates were willing to sling a little mud in the governor's direction, so much the better. If one of the other campaigns wanted to dig into the governor's past for evidence of incompetence or wrong-doing, good luck to them. In fact, if someone wanted to damage the governor's good name by fabricating some trumped-up charge against him, not a soul in the Stonewall campaign would have raised his voice to deny it. Thus did Governor Stonewall step boldly into the arena of the Democratic debate that fateful night in Florida. It is easy to be fearless when one is thirsting for defeat.

That evening the air was cooler than Florida's tropical reputation would have led one to expect, but in the auditorium where the debate was scheduled to take place the air conditioning was still cranked up at full blast. The governor went through the usual preliminaries—a last minute meeting with his staff to discuss logistics for the debate, a small amount of face powder applied to cut the gleam of his skin under the harsh spotlights, a little obligatory waving and hand-shaking with supporters in the audience just before taking the stage. And then the journalists and moderator took their places opposite the row of candidates—now reduced to five in number—and a hush fell over the crowd. The house lights dimmed, the stage lights came up, and the cameras began to roll.

For the first half-hour or so, the debate was rather a disappointment, at least from the governor's point of view. Regrettably, Yeager and Mondukis were still primarily focusing their attacks on each other, granting the other three candidates the decidedly mixed blessing of appearing to be above the fray but, at the same time, appearing to be somewhat irrelevant to the entire process at hand. Yeager accused Mondukis of influence-peddling, to which Mondukis responded by claiming that Yeager had ties to organized crime. Yeager then retaliated by painting his opponent as a puppet of special interest groups. By Scoop's estimation, Yeager was ahead, two unfounded accusations to one, and was therefore clearly winning the debate. The other candidates, meanwhile, tried to grab as much attention for themselves as they could in the midst of the ruckus. Howard Ruff once again presented his theory of trickle-down economics and Al Washington announced, to the surprise of absolutely no one, that he was opposed to drug use and felt that the government should do something to stop it.

The governor finally got his chance about forty-five minutes into the debate when the correspondent from CBS News asked him a question about crime. The governor responded with the usual prepared answer, emphasizing his belief that "criminals should be put in jail where they belong." And then he paused.

Scoop held his breath. While the rest of the governor's campaign staff was backstage, closely watching the proceedings on a video monitor, Scoop had positioned himself in a seat in the third row of the auditorium in order to be able to gauge the audience reaction first-hand. And now the time had come. Scoop looked at the governor on stage and for one brief moment their eyes met. Scoop nodded to him. The governor plunged ahead.

"As long as we're on the subject, I'd like to say something else," he began. "Seems to me an awful lot of the crime in these here cities of ours is being committed by one specific class of people. And every one of you, everyone out there listening, knows what I'm talking about. You can call it what you want, but the fact is it's true. And we give these people welfare, we give them food stamps…hell, we even give them our own jobs! We give them the same opportunities, the same shot at the American dream that everyone else has. And what do they do? They take drugs, they destroy their own neighborhoods, they have children out of wedlock when they're still in their teens, and they kill each other on the streets of our cities." And then came the clincher: "It's about time the American Negro learned how to behave in a civilized society."

There was a collective gasp from the audience. Scoop had never heard anything like it in his life—bouncing off the walls, reverberating through the air, the sound of a thousand people, all gasping in unison. Al Washington was the first one to lash back at the governor and one of the first words he used to do it was "racist." Ed Mondukis was up next, followed rapidly by Lloyd Yeager and Howard Ruff. Everyone seemed to be jockeying for a chance to express their outrage at the governor and, thereby, to make it clear to the national television audience that certainly they would never condone such a view. Even the panel of journalists couldn't resist getting in a few digs at the governor's expense. The governor, meanwhile, was completely unresponsive, never saying a word in his own defense or showing any outward sign of distress. Even as the debate proceeded and the audience took to hooting and heckling at the governor's every word, he remained calm, seemingly oblivious to the commotion he had caused. And if anyone had tuned in late to the debate, they would have seen the governor brimming with his usual laid-back confidence and good old boy charm and probably would have wondered why on earth the crowd was being so inexplicably hostile to this amiable Texan gentleman.

Meanwhile, Scoop could barely contain his glee. Sitting in the third row, he had to pinch himself hard several times in order to keep from bursting into laughter in the midst of the jeering crowd. It had worked perfectly, even better than he had hoped. And when the debate was over, the governor even had the audacity to step forward and, smiling, wave to the crowd, which responded with a round of enthusiastic booing. There was no doubt about it. The governor's campaign was over.

The ride back to the hotel had a celebratory feel to it, like a victorious sports team traveling home after having thoroughly beaten their rivals on the opponent's own turf. Reginald and the governor rode in the back seat of a rented limousine and monitored the newscasters' early responses to the debate on a portable television set. Scoop sat in the front seat next to the hired chauffeur. The television anchors seemed to be most offended by the use of the word "Negro," rather than "black" or even "African American." Scoop took particular pride in that. Various other racial epithets had been suggested by other members of the governor's staff and summarily dismissed; the goal, after all, was merely to sabotage the governor's campaign, not to start a full-blown riot. Scoop had finally suggested the use of the word "Negro," on the theory that it was offensive without being downright inflammatory. Besides, it was a word he hadn't heard anyone use in close to thirty years and it would serve to show how utterly out-of-touch with modern times the governor was.

The celebration continued once everyone arrived back at the hotel in Miami. Somebody ordered several bottles of champagne from room service and everyone toasted the demise of the campaign. Bret began the preparation of a final statement to show where the campaign stood financially and Scoop overheard Earl Jeeter on the phone, presumably with his wife, explaining how he would be coming home in a week or so. For Scoop's part, he commandeered a bottle of Dewar's from the hotel bar and retired to his room to conclude his own celebration in private.

It didn't last long. Not a half-hour had elapsed when there was a knock on Scoop's door. It was Earl Jeeter, his face looking even more worried than usual.

"You better get in here," he said, biting his lip. "Something's happening."

Scoop followed him down the carpeted hallway, past several anonymous numbered doors to Reginald's room. Reginald and Bret were already there, along with the governor, and all three of them were watching the television, their faces revealing varying degrees of concern and disbelief.

"Take a look," said Reginald numbly, as if in shock.

"Look," said Bret.

Scoop glanced at the television screen to see a reporter conducting a man-in-the-street interview. The subject of the interview looked to be about forty-five, a clean-shaven white man with an Operation Desert Storm baseball cap and a look of unsettling intensity in his eyes.

"...about goddamn time someone had the guts to say it," the man was saying. "I been out of work since last September and you better believe I been discriminated against. I'll tell you this for damn sure. If I was black, people'd be bending over backwards to give me a job." He paused to spit out a brown wad of chewing tobacco. "But the white man don't have no rights in this here country no more and it's..."

"You see?" asked Reginald, his voice fairly trembling. "Do you see what's happening?"

"Yeah, yeah, I see," said Scoop. "So it's a terrible thing when cousins marry. So what? I don't think we should be getting bent out of shape just because there's one mental deficient out there who's actually taking this shit seriously."

"But it's not just him," said Reginald. "Look." He clicked the remote control and the television flashed to a different channel. This time it was a pimply teenager in a Guns 'n' Roses T-shirt who was being interviewed.

"...like really awesome, man," the kid was saying. "I mean, this is, like, gonna be my first time votin' for the prez, y'know? And I think this Stonewall dude is, like, totally bitchin'. I mean, he just, like, says whatever he wants, man. Just like, y'know, Eminem. That's, like, totally cool, man."

"Oh, for God's sake," said Scoop. "I don't believe for a minute that..."

Reginald switched the channel again. This time it was an elderly woman with tainted blue hair and a genteel Southern drawl.

"Ah don't have nothin' 'gainst no colored folk," she was saying. "But ah do declare ah think they ought to learn themselves some manners. Ah think Mister Stonewall has a point when he says.."

"It's like this all over the dial," said Reginald, rapidly clicking the remote. "Every channel. The newscasters are giving him a thorough thrashing, to be sure, but some of the people seem to be supporting him."

"Okay, so the TV reporters have managed to dig up a cross section of genuine morons," said Scoop. "That's their job, to find unusual people to interview. Believe me, the print media is going to blow the lid off this thing. Just wait until the first editions hit the stands tomorrow morning."

But the reaction of the press wasn't quite what had been expected. Certainly the establishment newspapers—The New York Times, The Washington Post—thoroughly berated the governor for his statements. But the tabloids almost seemed to applaud his gutsiness. The Daily American proclaimed him "the only truly anti-establishment candidate in the presidential race." And even The New York Times had to admit that the governor appeared to be surging in the polls, having become the new hero of what they referred to as "the blue collar, Rush Limbaugh crowd."

Most of all, the governor's name had become a household word overnight. Within twenty-four hours of his having "dropped the bombshell," his name and face were plastered across the front pages of every newspaper in America. People either loved him or hated him, but everybody in the country knew who he was and everyone had an opinion of him. And while the governor's campaign staff lapsed into a state of utter shock and disarray, he continued to rise rapidly in the polls.

Until, on March 8th, Super Tuesday, the unthinkable finally happened. Governor Thurmond Stonewall began winning primaries.

6/ Illinois, March 15th

In the weeks following the Super Tuesday primaries, the Stonewall campaign raised close to a quarter of a million dollars. Naturally, most of that money did not come in the form of direct campaign contributions. Direct contributions, after all, were limited to a mere $1000 per person. Even contributions from political action committees were restricted to a $5000 maximum. So most of the funds that were being raised took the form of so-called "soft money."

Soft money was essentially a way to circumvent FEC regulations by hiding personal contributions, based on a loophole that limited only direct contributions to candidates but not contributions that indirectly helped their campaigns. An individual or corporation could therefore make a donation to the Democratic or Republican National Committees for any amount whatsoever and that contribution could be earmarked for a particular candidate. The money would then be channeled indirectly to the candidate through the party. The result was that big business and wealthy individuals were essentially able to buy the candidates of their choice and the money for the transaction would be laundered through the national party, a fortuitous arrangement for both candidate and contributor alike.

The fact that the governor's newfound popularity had led to an influx of campaign contributions was welcome news indeed, particularly seeing as how campaign expenditures were starting to go through the ozone. For, aside from the ridiculous amount of money which the campaign had needed to spend in order to appear to be competing in the Super Tuesday primaries, the Stonewall staff had now decided that it was time to produce a new television commercial.

Not that their first commercial hadn't been serving them in good stead. In fact, it had proven far more successful than anyone had imagined. With its grainy, out-of-focus cinematography and its almost inaudible soundtrack, it had been a strictly low-budget affair, shot in two days with a hand-held video camera for a cost of only a few thousand dollars. But the response to it had been surprisingly positive. An article in Advertising Age had referred to it as "refreshingly original" and "truly cutting edge." The Village Voice claimed that it was "the first campaign commercial designed for the YouTube generation." And a commentator for The New York Review of Books called it "a post-modernist statement about the deliberate ambiguity of the human condition" and "the epitome of minimalist ennui." The commercial had even gone on to win several major advertising awards, turning its director into a celebrity overnight and drawing national media attention to the release of his newest feature-length work, this one entitled *Annie Does Austin.*

Be that as it may, the fact that the campaign was already almost six months old and had only produced the one television commercial was beginning to look a little suspicious, or at least so Reginald feared. Hence, Reginald decided that they needed to produce another one quickly. But that would take money and money was the one thing the campaign staff didn't want to part with.

"What about corruption?" Reginald asked one night. "Governor, have you ever been involved in any business transactions which might be characterized as, shall we say, unsavory?"

"Heh?" said the governor. "What do you mean, unsavory?"

"I mean dishonest, disreputable, unscrupulous?"

"Certainly not!" the governor shot back. "Every business deal I've ever conducted has been completely above board."

"Christ, here we go again," said Scoop.

They were sitting in a hotel room in Chicago the week before the Illinois primary, surrounded by vaguely worded position papers and fast food packaging. In a corner of the room, a television set tuned to CNN provided a soundtrack of breaking news and financial reports.

"What about bribes?" asked Scoop. "Have you ever taken a bribe, Governor? Even a little one?"

The governor glared at him. "I won't even dignify that question with a response."

"No, of course not," said Scoop. "What was I thinking? God knows, you're a saint, Governor. Politics is a dirty business, but you of course are completely clean. Everybody's either screwing or getting screwed and you've somehow managed to hang on to your virginity. You've somehow managed to stay above the fray, a symbol of purity and integrity in government, a hero for our time." Scoop shook his head in disbelief. "You're only motivation is to serve the people, right? Selfless dedication, never a thought for yourself. Well, God bless you, Governor. God bless you. Can you ever forgive me for thinking otherwise?"

"You know, I'm starting to get pretty goddamn sick and tired of you and your self-righteous attitude, boy," said the governor. "Last time I looked you were right down here in the gutter with the rest of us. So why don't you do us all a goddamn favor and turn off the holier-than-thou bullshit?"

"Gentlemen, please," said Reginald, rubbing the exhaustion from his eyes. "Fighting amongst ourselves is counterproductive. Let's attempt to focus all our energies on bringing this campaign to a speedy conclusion, shall we?"

"That's what I'm *trying* to do," said Scoop. "But it would help if we could get a little cooperation here. Something to *go* on. Anything."

"Well what the hell do you want me to do, boy?" asked the governor. "You want me to start making stuff up? Maybe invent some kind of shady business deal for you to use? Say that something happened when it didn't? Is that what you want?"

Reginald looked up. "Invent...?"

"Christ, I give up," said Scoop. "You know what it is? You know what I really think it is? You're enjoying this, aren't you? Part of you is really enjoying this. All the media attention, your name all over the fucking newspapers. You're enjoying it. Even as the nooses are tightening around our fucking necks, you're really enjoying it."

"Go to hell," said the governor.

"Wait a minute," said Reginald. "Back up a bit. The governor said something very intelligent there."

"That would be the first time," said Scoop.

"When?" said the governor. "I said something? What?"

"About inventing a shady business deal," said Reginald. "Making something up that never happened."

"Did I say that?"

"Think about it," continued Reginald. "It would solve a lot

of problems. I mean, even if we had an actual business transaction from the governor's past that was, shall we say, less than completely scrupulous, it would be extremely difficult to prove. Doubtless there would be no trail of paperwork to demonstrate what had transpired and any of the other parties that had been involved would be sure to deny it most strenuously. And if there were no way to prove that it had happened, the governor would have no realistic motive for coming forward on the subject, now would he?

"But," continued Reginald, clearly warming to his subject, "what if we were to concoct a situation of our own device? We could create the paper trail ourselves. That would be easy enough, wouldn't it, Bret?"

"Easy enough," agreed Bret.

"But who would the governor be doing the deal *with*?" asked Earl, biting his lip. "I mean, even if we could demonstrate it on paper, we'd still need the cooperation of an outside party."

Reginald smiled in a self-satisfied way. "I'm sure we'll have no problem finding someone who's willing to cooperate. Every lobbyist, every corporation, every PAC, every major campaign contributor in the country is looking for an 'in' with the candidate. It's happening in every campaign. But the financial relationships are usually implicit. There's no *quid pro quo* that anyone can point a finger at, nothing tangible that anyone can really get their hands on. All we need do is take the financial relationships that already exist and make them explicit. Take them out of the shadows and into the light of day, as it were."

"Sure," said Scoop, his expression becoming more intense as the ideas began churning in his head. "It should be easy to pull off. We set up the deal, make the pitch, and wait for the first contributor to take the bait. It'll be like..." He searched for a word to approximate the situation. "...entrapment."

"Perhaps 'reverse entrapment' would be a more accurate description," asserted Reginald, "since it's our own man we're trying to entrap."

"But wouldn't the other guy still deny it?" the governor chimed in, not wanting to be left out of the conversation entirely.

"Not if he couldn't," said Scoop. "Not if we had it on tape. Just like the police do when they're trying to set someone up. Videotape the whole thing."

"And then send the tape to the Yeager campaign," said Reginald.

"Anonymously," added Bret.

"Anonymously," agreed Reginald.

And so the gears were set in motion. The plot, as suggested by Bret, was a fairly commonplace election year maneuver, in which a corporation would circumvent the FEC's limits on campaign contributions by dispensing the money through its employees. For example, if a company employed five hundred people and wanted to make a contribution of $100,000, it would simply instruct each of its employees to make a personal contribution of two hundred dollars, an amount well within FEC guidelines. The company would then include an extra two hundred dollars in each employee's next paycheck, ostensibly as overtime pay or a bonus, but really to compensate them. This was fairly typical and the Stonewall campaign had conducted such transactions with numerous corporations since the campaign had begun. But they were always carried out with a wink and a nod, neither party fully acknowledging what they were doing. Now, the Stonewall campaign was going to manufacture a smoking gun. They were going to produce a videotape in which the governor explicitly suggested such an arrangement to a contributor. It would, everyone agreed, be devastating to the campaign.

The target that Reginald and Bret finally chose was George Epstein, president of one of the largest banks in Illinois. Epstein had scheduled a private meeting with the governor, to take place just two days before the primary. That gave Scoop and Earl enough time to buy a video camera and some recording equipment, including several small microphones that could be easily concealed. Scoop drilled a hole in the adjoining wall between Reginald's room and the governor's while Earl set up a table in the governor's room, directly in front of the hole. The governor would be seated at the table when Epstein entered the room and would beckon the unsuspecting banker to join him, so that both of them would be easily within range of the camera. Scoop and Earl role-played the scene several times and Reginald concluded that no one would have had difficulty identifying the participants from the resultant videotapes.

The sound turned out to be a trickier problem. Scoop tried a number of different microphones and none of them proved satisfactory. Either they were too weak, and hence were incapable of picking up both of the speakers clearly, or they were too powerful and picked up extraneous noises, the sounds of the man across the hall snoring or the couple upstairs having sex, indistinguishable from the ones they had heard through the thin walls of some of the seedier hotels in which they had stayed (proving, Scoop noted with some interest, that couples of all socio-economic backgrounds make approximately the same noises while screwing).

Scoop had finally settled on the microphone he thought worked best and was prepared to tape it to the underside of the governor's table, when Earl raised the possibility of Epstein's moving about the room.

"What if he does?" asked Scoop,

"He'd walk right out of microphone range," said Earl. "If that's the only microphone we've got hooked up and he wanders away from the table…"

"If he wanders away from the table, he'll be out of camera range, too," said Scoop. "So what the hell are we supposed to do?"

"Earl has a legitimate point, Scoop," Reginald interceded. "It isn't that important for both subjects to be on camera every minute. But we want to be assured that we don't miss a single word of their exchange."

"Great," said Scoop. "So what do we do? Put microphones all over the goddamn room? Christ, we don't know what the hell we're doing here. Can't we hire a professional to handle this?"

Bret looked up sharply. "Negative," he said. "I'm afraid that simply wouldn't do. We just can't afford it. The profit margin is far too tight as it is. Besides, the CIA does this sort of thing all the time. It can't be *too* difficult."

"We can handle this," said Reginald. He thought for a moment. "What if we had the governor wear a wire?"

"You mean he'd be carrying the microphone himself?" said Earl. "Taping himself while he sets himself up?"

"Great," grumbled the governor. "Like being a pallbearer at my own damn funeral."

"Well, it would solve certain fundamental problems," said

Reginald. "That way if our Mr. Epstein begins strolling about the room, you can stay by his side."

"What if he goes to take a leak?" asked the governor sarcastically. "Am I supposed to follow him into the goddamn crapper?"

Reginald smiled in a way that stopped just short of condescension. "I don't think that will be necessary, Governor."

"On the other hand," said Scoop, "if you did follow him into the crapper, that would sabotage the campaign for sure."

"Don't even *think* about it, boy."

So the governor was fitted with a small microphone which he wore underneath his shirt, secured to his chest with adhesive tape. And all the equipment was in place, the governor seated at his table and Scoop, Earl, and the Worthington brothers positioned in Reginald's room, the video camera and tape recorder set before them on tables they had each dragged in from their own respective rooms, when the esteemed George Epstein arrived for his allegedly private audience with the governor.

"Come in," shouted the governor in response to the knock on his door.

The volume and suddenness of his voice startled Reginald, who was monitoring the scene through a pair of headphones. "He's in," he reported to the others.

Scoop checked the image being filmed by the video camera through the hole in the wall. "Okay, Epstein is sitting down at the table. They're both within camera range."

"Perfect," Reginald whispered.

Epstein and the governor began with small talk: the weather, the start of spring training, an offhand comment the president had made to the press earlier that week.

"What are they saying?" insisted Earl.

"Nothing of substance yet," said Reginald. "Shh."

"You seem to have turned a few heads, Governor," said Epstein. "Beaten the odds, that's for sure."

The governor feigned modesty. "Just telling it like I see it. Somebody's got to have the guts to shoot from the hip."

"Yes," said Epstein. "And I understand you've been quite a friend to the banking industry down there in Texas, haven't you?"

"I believe banks are the cornerstone of society," the governor replied. "A community is only as strong as its banks, that's what I always say."

"I couldn't agree with you more," said Epstein. He glanced towards the window. "Say, you've got quite a view of downtown."

"Heh?"

Epstein stood and walked towards the window. Downtown Chicago was spread before him like a scale model on an architect's drawing table. "Yes indeed, quite a..." He turned to find the governor facing him, roughly half an inch away.

"Is there something wrong, Governor?"

"Wrong?" said the governor. "No, siree. Not a thing. What could possibly be wrong?"

Epstein took a half-step to the right. The governor stepped to the left, blocking him. Epstein took a step back to the left. The governor mirrored his action like a well-trained dance partner.

"Governor, are you sure there isn't something wrong?"

"Heh? What do you mean, wrong?"

"What the hell is going on?" asked Earl.

"Can't tell," said Scoop. "They're both out of camera range. Reg?"

"Nothing yet," said Reginald. "Wait. I think that's it. Epstein just said something about a contribution. This is the opening we've been waiting for."

And then, all at once, Reginald's face registered confusion.

"What is it?" asked Scoop. "What's happening?"

"I'm not sure," said Reginald, clearly perplexed. "It sounds like the governor...that is to say, the governor appears to be...singing."

"Singing?" said Scoop. "What do you mean, singing? What the hell is he singing?"

Reginald listened intently for a moment. "Something about... something about being too sexy." he said. "For his cat."

"He's too silly for his cat?"

"No, *sexy*," said Reginald. "He's too *sexy* for his cat." Reginald stopped to listen again. "Now it's his shirt. He's too sexy for his shirt."

"What the hell are you talking about?" said Earl. "The governor is too sexy for his shirt? What do you mean, he's too sexy for his shirt?"

"Look, don't blame me," Reginald shot back, his voice a hoarse whisper. "I'm just telling you what he's saying."

"But it doesn't make any *sense*," Earl protested. "What does that mean, he's too sexy for his shirt?"

"Oh, no," said Scoop as realization began to dawn on him. "Does anyone know if the governor has any fillings?"

"Fillings?" asked Bret.

"Wait, something's happening," said Reginald. "He's saying something else now."

"What?" asked Earl. "What?"

"He's evidently instructing Epstein to refrain from touching something," said Reginald.

"What?"

"'Can't touch this,'" said Reginald. "He keeps repeating that one statement over and over. I'm quite certain of it. 'Can't touch this.' He's being somewhat vague about the exact nature of the object in question, but he's nonetheless quite adamant about the request."

"Reg, for Christ's sake, it's the *radio*," said Scoop.

"Wait, it's changing again," said Reginald. "He's saying something else. A mulatto…an albino…a mosquito…no, that can't be right."

"Reg, will you turn the damn tape recorder *off?*" said Scoop.

By the end of the day, the Stonewall campaign had obtained a commitment from George Epstein for a total of $120,000 in campaign contributions. They also had in their possession a rather lengthy videotape of an unoccupied table sitting in the governor's hotel room and roughly thirty minutes of music recorded from WKLB, Chicago's up-and-coming top-forty radio station, with more music, less talk, and free jackpot giveaways every hour on the hour. "Listen for your chance to win on the station that gives you more hits more of the time…"

It was a few nights later and the governor was sound asleep when the telephone in his hotel room rang. He picked it up on the third ring.

"Stonewall?" came the voice. "This is Howard Ruff."

The unexpected sound of his opponent's voice startled the governor from his drowsiness.

"Howard. What can I do for you?" The governor squinted at the clock on his bedside table. It was well past 2 AM.

"Well, Thurmond, I've got some news for you," said Ruff. "I'm pulling out of the race tomorrow. Thought you might like to know. There'll be a press conference first thing tomorrow morning."

For a moment, the governor wondered if he was dreaming, or maybe if this was a crank call. "Pulling out, eh? What's the matter, Howard? Can't take the heat?"

There was a short chortle on the line. "Nah, I finally realized I'm just not cut out for politics. Too many asses you've got to kiss, too many times you've got to bite your tongue instead of saying what's really on your mind. You know what I mean. I'm just plain sick of it, Thurmond. And when you beat the crap out of me in Illinois...well, that was the last straw. Nah, politics just isn't my bag. Give me a life in the private sector any day of the week."

The governor tried to think of something appropriate to say. "Well, we'll miss you, Howard. You made it a more interesting race, that's for damn sure."

"Thanks, Thurm. Nice of you to say so. Listen, I'd like to make a contribution to your campaign. Say, about $150,000?"

The governor shut his eyes. Crap. Where the hell was a tape recorder when you needed one?

"Well, that's mighty white of you, Howard. I really appreciate you swinging your support to my campaign."

Ruff laughed. "Now just hold on a minute there, cowboy. I didn't say anything about swinging my support your way. As far as I'm concerned, my electoral votes are still up for grabs. I'm not sure what I'm going to be asking for them yet. Maybe I'll just hang onto them for a while and see what kind of offers I get. No, all I'm talking about is a contribution. And I'm contributing the same amount to the Yeager and Mondukis campaigns, too."

The governor sat up in bed. "You're contributing the same amount of money to all our campaigns?"

"Hell, yes. That way I'll have a fix in no matter which one of you bastards wins." Ruff began chuckling. "You know, it finally occurred to me. Who needs all this bullshit? The press conferences, the fundraisers, all the goddamn questions. Who the hell needs it? I finally got to thinking. Why the hell would I want to become president when I can just buy myself one?"

He was still laughing when the governor hung up.

7/ Michigan, March 26th

To Scoop, there had always been something downright absurd about the primary process. What with the campaign hurtling from city to city at breakneck speed, maneuvering its way through a bewildering patchwork of state primary laws, each one more complex and nonsensical than the one before, it was no wonder the voters had difficulty piecing together a coherent view of the candidates' positions—assuming, of course, that some of the candidates actually had coherent positions. It seemed, at best, a rather haphazard way for a people to choose its leader.

More than anything else, Scoop saw the campaign as a test of physical endurance, a marathon race in which the voters got to see how well the candidates were capable of performing under pressure, with bad food in their stomachs and only two hours of sleep behind them. And as the candidates raced from one end of the country to the other, their nerves and stamina pushed ever closer to the limits of human capacity, the voters watched the evening news expectantly, licking their lips in anticipation, waiting for each candidate in turn to stumble and fall. And stumble they would—with each gaffe and misjudged position, with each scandal and misstatement, they would fall by the wayside, the contemptuous jeers of the public ringing in their ears. Until, finally, only a single runner remained, aching and weary and covered with the grime of the road. But by then he had become damaged goods in the eyes of the public, his weaknesses too apparent, his flaws too blatantly exposed. So rather than greeting him as a hero, he would be judged the lesser of evils, at best a merely half-decent choice from a pack of inferior alternatives. And as he somehow, miraculously, limped across the finish line, the voters would not greet him with the cheers of victory. By that point, the most enthusiastic response they would be able to muster would be a shrug of the shoulders as they clicked the television remote control.

As for Scoop's own role, he liked to think of himself as a supporting player in a traveling road show, maybe a particularly amateurish production of *The Fantasticks* or *Man of La Mancha*. Every few days he and his touring company would pull into another town, hang their posters on every available lamp post and telephone pole, hastily assemble their stage and deliver their performance. And then, having had their opportunity to strut and fret their hour, and just as the first reviews began appearing in the local papers, they would pack their bags, pull up their stakes, and hurriedly depart for the next stop on their tour. It was a decidedly whimsical view and Scoop was becoming increasingly fond of whimsy, particularly seeing as he was in the process of polishing off his fourth Dewar's.

He slid the glass of half-melted ice cubes across the top of the bar towards the bartender. "Another," he grumbled shortly.

He was sitting in the bar of a hotel in Detroit. He couldn't remember the name of the hotel and he sincerely hoped, with the help of a few more drinks, to forget the name of the city as well. The room was identical to the bars of a hundred other hotels he had been in throughout the country—fake wood paneling, imitation brass railings, racks of empty glasses suspended upside down from the ceiling above the bartender's head. The bartender was a young, well-dressed black man, evidently a local college student trying to pick up a few extra bucks by working at night. Scoop had taken a liking to him earlier in the evening when he had refilled Scoop's glass quickly and hadn't tried to make conversation. Scoop didn't like idle chatter and he particularly wasn't in the mood for it tonight.

It had been one hell of a day. In the afternoon, the governor had had an appointment to meet with Jake Chancy, head of one of the largest and most powerful labor unions in the country. Chancy was currently involved in a battle with a young upstart named Trent Cindler for control of the union and was looking to gain some favorable press by rubbing elbows with a presidential candidate. Scoop figured that Chancy had also wanted to demonstrate that he was still the one who wielded the most clout in the union by endorsing said candidate.

So naturally the entire staff of the Stonewall campaign had spent the better part of the morning in conference, trying to concoct a way to sabotage the afternoon meeting and thereby avoid the endorsement. Suggestions ranged from having the governor pour hot coffee in Chancy's lap to taking a dump on his shoes. The plan that was finally adopted was considerably less dramatic. The governor was simply going to refuse the endorsement and, to add insult to injury, accuse Chancy of being a crook, a not terribly controversial statement for anyone familiar with Chancy's record as leader of the union. The plan proceeded without a hitch and, sure enough, Chancy burst out of the meeting just three minutes after it had begun, red-faced and fuming and vowing to pledge the union's support to Ed Mondukis. Score one for our side, thought Scoop.

Unfortunately, finding the kind of privacy necessary to discuss such a ploy was becoming increasingly difficult. It wasn't just that the campaign was attracting more and more press attention, as if that weren't bad enough. No, now there were also the goddamn Secret Service agents to worry about. They were everywhere, constantly underfoot— lurking in the corners of the governor's hotel room, walking in the governor's shadow wherever he went, even standing next to the urinal when he took a leak. With their identical dark suits, walkie-talkies, and radio receivers shoved in their ears, they were practically indistinguishable, like clones or robots that had all marched off the same assembly line. During his first presidential campaign, years ago, Scoop had actually made an attempt to learn their names. Now he was in the habit of calling all of them "Fred," even the women. After all, it didn't much matter what the hell he called them or what he said to them. Their behavior seemed to be pre-programmed, like drones in the same hive, all buzzing mindlessly around the queen. Not surprisingly, the governor actually found their presence exciting, contributing as it did to his sense of self-importance. To Scoop, they were nothing but an annoyance.

Scoop took a long gulp of Dewar's. What the hell was wrong with him? He should be used to putting up with the Secret Service by now. Why was he feeling so damned uneasy? It was something about the campaign, he knew. No, it was *everything* about the campaign. Not one thing had gone the way it was supposed to since the governor had thrown his hat into the ring. Every plan had backfired, every calculation had produced totally the wrong result. The campaign should have been over a month ago. Instead, the governor was more popular now than he had ever been. In all the times that Scoop and the Worthingtons had worked the scam, that had never happened before.

But it was more than that. It was the *kind* of support that the governor was attracting that bothered Scoop. Since his comments at the Florida debate earlier that month, the governor had begun receiving letters of support from white supremacists across the country. They would tell the governor how great it was to have "one of them" in the race for the presidency and then sign the note with expressions like "White Power" or "KKK Forever." Many of the letters had personal checks enclosed and the governor had also received a large donation from Aryan Nation. One group had even enclosed a color snapshot of themselves dressed in sheets, a cross burning in the background, like a picture postcard from hell.

In addition, groups of skinheads had started showing up at the governor's rallies, their black leather jackets emblazoned with Nazi swastikas. Scoop had been momentarily startled, not merely by their presence but by how young they were; their faces were barely accustomed to the touch of a shaving razor, but the hatred in their eyes seemed incongruously adult. With their shaved heads and Doc Marten boots, they might almost have been comical, a bunch of teenagers on their way to a costume party. But the political emblem with which they chose to adorn themselves, with its attendant associations of horror and suffering, agony and despair, was enough to have a sobering effect even on one as flippantly cynical as Scoop.

In fact, as a Jew, perhaps the symbol was even more disturbing to Scoop. He remembered when he was a child and his parents used to tell him stories about the Holocaust, about all the uncles and aunts and cousins he would have had if they hadn't been exterminated in places with names like Dachau and Treblinka and Bergen-Belsen, and about how lucky his parents were to have been living in America at the time. He remembered how much the stories used to scare him, filling his child's mind with worry and barely imagined horrors and a feeling of dread that was intensified by the fact that, unlike all his other usual childhood frights, his parents seemed to actually *share* this fear. This wasn't just another fantasy boogeyman hiding under the bed that could be easily dispelled with one comforting kiss from his mother, but something that was very real or at least had been not so long ago. He hadn't known until then that adults could be afraid of things too and the realization sent tremors of instability through the very foundations of his tiny, child's universe.

And now here he was, working for the candidate who was fast becoming the latest darling of the neo-Nazi lunatic fringe. Whatever would Mom and Dad say? he snickered.

What the hell was going on? When did politics get so fucking crazy? And what was *he* doing there in the middle of it all? He stared dumbly into his drink, as if somehow expecting to find the answers concealed within the ice cubes, the way a gypsy fortune teller reads prophecies in a cup of tea leaves.

There was a time when this would have been exciting to Scoop— working on a presidential campaign, his candidate rising steadily in the polls. Of course, in those days Scoop would never have been associated with a sleazebag like Thurmond Stonewall. No, he would have devoted himself to working for a candidate with principles, with ideals, someone who was truly dedicated to blazing a new path for the country. Someone who would help the needy and feed the hungry and all that shit. Scoop chuckled to himself as he took another drink, the liquor sloppily wetting his upper lip. Well, it was bound to happen. Yep, another attack of conscience, a blast from the past, another golden fucking oldie, just when he thought he had finally outgrown them. But no, here it was, right on schedule. At least once every campaign, no getting around it. What was that expression he had heard once? Scratch a cynic and you'll find a frustrated idealist? Well, fuck that shit.

Still, the memories were irresistible. Scoop closed his eyes and for a moment he was back in college, sitting cross-legged on the floor of his dorm room, stuffing envelopes for Eugene McCarthy, with Jefferson Airplane or the Strawberry Alarm Clock playing on the stereo and the hint of cannabis scenting the air. Briefly, unexpectedly, a woman's face flashed before him.

Christ, he thought, not her. He hadn't thought of her in years. A series of pictures and sounds and feelings ran through him like an electric shock. It was like watching a sentimental old movie in fast motion, a movie with whose plot he was so familiar he had no need to slow it down in order to follow it. One scene in particular stood out in his mind—the two of them making love in her dorm room, the creaking of the bed, the sound of kids talking and laughing out in the hall, the smell of her hair like wild juniper berries, the physical sensations of sweat and exertion and the uncanny aching pleasure of sexual stimulation, the Byrds' "Eight Miles High" wafting in from the room next door.

Shit. What the hell was her name? Lisa something-or-other…

"Gin on the rocks." It was definitely a woman's voice, but flat and jaded, as if every trace of femininity had been pounded out of it with a mallet. Scoop looked up. Who the hell drinks gin on the rocks?

She was standing at the bar, just two feet away from him. Scoop guessed her to be in her early thirties. She was dressed simply but professionally in a mid-length dress of dark blue. Scoop noticed that it clung to her rather loosely and was cut high enough to conceal even a trace of cleavage.

"Gin on the rocks," he repeated. "You trying to punish yourself?"

The woman removed a pack of cigarettes from her purse without even glancing in his direction. "I used to drink martinis dry. Then I started drinking them *very* dry. Then I finally decided to quit kidding myself and just go for the gin. As if anyone really drinks martinis for the vermouth."

"I always thought it was for the olive," said Scoop. "I don't think I've ever seen a woman drink straight gin."

At this she finally turned to face him, the glass in her hand. She met his eyes directly, almost challengingly, and without losing eye contact she took a long gulp of her drink. "Stick around. Maybe you'll learn something."

Scoop noticed her eyes, large and very green, and the dark brown hair that tumbled to her shoulders in waves. Okay, he thought. You've got my attention.

"You from around here?" Scoop asked.

The woman gave him a patronizing smirk and shook her head. "Now that's not a very original line, is it? Let me guess. You haven't tried picking up a woman in a bar for a long time, right?"

Is that what he was trying to do? Scoop wasn't sure. Maybe he was.

"I guess asking what a nice girl like you is doing in a place like this is out of the question then, eh?" said Scoop.

"My, you are up on all the classics, aren't you?" said the woman. "Sounds like you've memorized the whole manual, front to back. But don't you know you're supposed to offer a lady a light when she takes out a cigarette?" She moved closer, waving the still unlit cigarette before him.

Scoop picked up a book of matches from the bar, lit one and held it out towards her. The woman pulled a lighter from her purse and lit the cigarette herself. "Thanks," she said, breathing a cloud of smoke in his direction.

Scoop forced a smirk and shook out the match. "Okay, I'll guess. I'd say you're not from around here. I'd say you're in town for the campaign. I'll also go out on a limb and say you just had a lousy day and decided to bust the balls of the first guy you ran into. How am I doing so far?"

For a moment, a smile that might actually have been genuine flashed across the woman's face. But it evaporated instantly, leading Scoop to question whether he had seen it in the first place or if it had just been a trick of the light. "You must be psychic," she said. "Right on all three counts. As a matter of fact, I'm covering the Stonewall campaign."

A reporter, thought Scoop. Should have known. "Really," he said. "How interesting." He took a long, slow sip of Dewar's and eyed her closely. "And what is your informed opinion of the esteemed governor from Texas? Has he won you over yet with his cowboy drawl and his good old boy country charm?"

The woman studied her drink. "He's an exciting man,' she said seriously. "Certainly the only candidate in the race worth writing about. The others are old news, boring as hell. Stonewall's the only one who's bringing any life to the campaign. He's different, he's controversial. Everybody's talking about him. He's got style, he's got charisma. He's his own man. As far as I'm concerned, he's the only one worth watching."

Scoop searched her face for a trace of sarcasm. He couldn't find any, but somehow he knew it was there just the same. "Something tells me you're not being...shall we say, completely genuine with me."

The woman looked up and, with a quick jerk of her neck, threw back her hair. It returned to its resting place a moment later, like waves to the shore. "Okay," she said. "What if I told you I thought the governor was a narrow-minded, race-baiting son of a bitch who's using every slimy political trick in the book to get elected? He's shallow and two-faced, he doesn't give a damn about the rights of women or minorities, and his campaign is morally and intellectually bankrupt. What if I told you that?"

Scoop smirked. "At least then I'd say you were being honest. What if I told you that I was just talking to the governor, not two hours ago?"

The woman shrugged and turned back towards the bar. "What if you did? What if you told me you worked on the governor's campaign? What if you told me you were someone he took into his confidence, a member of his inner circle—his press secretary, say? What if you told me you were Joel Heidelman—'Scoop' Heidelman to your friends?" She took a long drag on her cigarette. "What if you did?"

Shit, thought Scoop. He must be getting stupid in his old age, talking to this woman for ten whole minutes and never even realizing he was being played. He should cut off the conversation right then and there, he told himself. Right that second. But there was something that held him there, held him to the spot, unable to break away. Later, he would think back to that night and wish he had trusted his instincts, had done what his better judgment had advised him. But for the moment, drunk on scotch and self-pity and the smell of her perfume, walking away didn't seem an act of which he was even capable.

"It appears you have me at a disadvantage," he said.

"Good, she replied. "Just the way I like it."

It had been a long time since Scoop had felt attracted to a woman. Mostly, he was either too busy or too drunk to bother thinking about it. But there was something he found undeniably exciting about *this* woman— something about her presence, about the self-assured way she stood and moved, something he couldn't quite put his finger on, like a charge of electricity that hung around her. He again noticed the way she was dressed—modestly, in an outfit that was neither too tight nor too short for anyone's grandmother to consider inappropriate. Scoop guessed that she probably dressed that way often. In order to be taken seriously as a journalist, perhaps she had learned to suppress her womanliness, to conceal any trace of sexuality in her manner of dress or tone of voice. But despite her best efforts, she was unable to hide it. Her sensuousness filled the room like the light from a candle.

Of course, thought Scoop, he was probably perceiving her precisely as she wanted him to. All part of the game, after all. But then again, so what? What difference did it make? He tried to deduce what her figure looked like beneath the dress.

"So are you going to tell me who you are?" asked Scoop. "Or do I have to go back to playing twenty questions?"

The woman turned to face him again. "Just waiting for you to ask," she said. "Roman. Sarah Roman. I'm a reporter for Profile Magazine"

"Ah, yes. Profile Magazine." Scoop smiled, for the first time feeling as if he had the upper hand in the conversation. "Isn't that the glossy magazine they sell at supermarket checkout counters? The one that ran the exclusive photos of Paris Hilton skinny-dipping? Let's see, I believe your lead story last week was a hard-hitting investigative report on Lindsay Lohan, wasn't it?"

Scoop noticed a slight stiffening of her spine. "First of all, it isn't only sold in supermarkets. And secondly, Profile Magazine happens to be an important source of information for millions of Americans. For many, it's their *primary* source of information. Besides, I don't think your candidate is proposing any complex foreign policy initiatives that are beyond the intellectual scope of my magazine's readers, is he? If so, I haven't heard about it."

Scoop smiled and raised his glass in mock salute. "Touché, Ms. Roman. Touché."

Sarah finished the last of her gin and replaced the glass on the bar. "And on that note, I'd best be going. It's been a pleasure, Mr. Heidelman."

Scoop raised his eyebrows. "That's it? Nothing more?"

"What do you mean?" she asked, her face a mask of innocence.

"Aren't you going to ask for an exclusive interview with the governor?" said Scoop. "That is what this whole scene was about, wasn't it? That's why you picked me out from across the room and came over to have a drink with me."

Sarah smiled, almost condescendingly. "Of course I'd like an interview. But you wouldn't give it to me now even if I asked you for it, would you?"

"No," said Scoop.

"No," Sarah repeated. "I knew you wouldn't. Not yet. But you will. Eventually. Trust me, I have an instinct about these things." She picked her cigarettes off the bar and dropped them into her purse. "In the meantime, good luck in the primary. See you in Wisconsin, Scoop."

The following day, editorials in newspapers around the country were singing the praises of Thurmond Stonewall. Even The New York Times, ordinarily one of the governor's harshest critics, was applauding his rejection of the endorsement from labor leader Jake Chancy. Citing Chancy's long history of criminal activities and his rumored association with organized crime, The Times hailed Stonewall for his integrity and for demonstrating that, as they put it, "he is not a puppet of any special interest group."

In a related development, Chancy's rival for control of the union, Trent Cindler, held a press conference that afternoon. Cindler also applauded the governor's action, while blasting Ed Mondukis for accepting Chancy's endorsement. In addition, Cindler stated that it was time for the union's rank and file to reject Chancy's leadership and, as a show of strength, he encouraged all union members to vote for Stonewall instead of Mondukis in the primary.

The rank and file reacted to Cindler's request with enthusiasm, the primary thus transformed into what was more a referendum on Chancy's leadership of the union than a contest between presidential candidates. And when the dust settled, Cindler had clearly won. Exit polls showed that a full 80% of union members had voted for Stonewall over Mondukis, helping to boost the governor to a victory in the Michigan primary.

The big loser in the election was Reverend Al Washington, who had spent ten years in the Detroit area and was counting on a big win in Michigan to provide a much needed boost to his faltering campaign. When that boost failed to materialize, Washington withdrew from the race and threw his support behind Ed Mondukis.

It was now a three-way race.

8/ Wisconsin, April 5th

The idea came to Reginald in a flash and he couldn't wait to tell someone.

"Butz!" he shouted as he burst into the governor's hotel room, where the rest of the campaign staff was already assembled for the morning meeting.

"You watch your mouth, boy," said the governor. "I don't care if you are my campaign manager. Nobody calls me that and gets away with it."

"No," said Reginald. "I mean Earl Butz. Surely you recall Earl Butz, Governor. Secretary of—"

"—Agriculture under the Carter administration," finished Bret. "Of course. It's perfect."

"What?" said the governor. "What's perfect?"

"Do you recall how Earl Butz left office, Governor?" said Reginald. "It was all due to a joke he told."

"Something about tight pussy and a warm place to shit, wasn't it?" asked Scoop.

"Precisely," said Reginald. "As I recall, he told the joke to a fellow passenger during a plane trip and it wound up being reported in Rolling Stone. There was a public outcry and within the month he was…shall we say, no longer on the government payroll."

"Of course," said Scoop. "It's so simple. Why didn't we think of it before? Here we've been wasting our time planting time bombs in the governor's position papers, when we know damn well nobody reads that shit anyway. But a joke—that's a different story. Nothing spreads across the country faster than a joke. That's the answer!"

"Just imagine," said Reginald, a faraway look in his eyes, "one day the governor makes an offensive joke within earshot of a journalist. The next day it's being repeated around every water cooler of every office in America. By the end of the week, the governor's out of the race." Reginald swept his eyes over everyone in the room. "Gentlemen, all we need is one *killer joke!*"

So everybody filled their coffee cups and pulled their chairs into a tight semi-circle around the couch. They sat with pens or pencils grasped tightly in their hands and yellow legal pads resting in their laps, waiting to scribble down all the brilliance that would no doubt result from their brainstorming.

"All right, gentlemen," Reginald began when he was sure everyone was settled, "who has a joke?"

An embarrassingly long period of silence passed as blank stares were exchanged around the circle.

"Come now, gentlemen," prompted Reginald, "don't be shy. Surely someone must know a joke."

More blank stares. The only sound was the ticking of the governor's travel alarm clock on the bedside table.

"Oh for God's sake," said Reginald, exasperated. "I can't believe none of us knows a single joke!"

"Never had much of a head for jokes," said the governor seriously, his face strained with concentration. "I mean, I like to laugh at them, just can't ever remember the goddamn punch lines. Goes in one ear and out the other, I reckon."

"Why don't you go first?" Earl whined to Reginald. "Get us started."

"What? Oh, all right..." Reginald sat up in his chair and took a deep breath. "Let's see now...uh..."

Several more moments of silence passed, everyone's eyes fixed on Reginald.

"Well for God's sake," Reginald finally snapped, "I can't think of any with all of you staring at me!"

"Wait!" said Earl. "I have one! Knock, knock. Who's there?"

"A knock-knock joke?" said Scoop. "We're going to have the governor tell a knock-knock joke?"

"What's wrong with that?" demanded Earl.

"It's stupid, that's what's wrong with it!" said Scoop. "Nobody tells knock-knock jokes!"

"I tell them all the time," said Earl. "To my daughter."

"Your daughter's five years old!" said Scoop.

"Gentlemen, please," said Reginald. "This is a brainstorming session. The idea is to be creative, not critical."

"Not critical," agreed Bret.

"Precisely," said Reginald. "So let's simply toss out whatever ideas we have and write them all down. Then later on we can refer back to our notes and be more selective. Agreed? All right then. Earl, please proceed."

Earl nodded with great seriousness. "Knock knock. Who's there? Jose. Jose who?" He sang the last part to the tune of the national anthem. "Jose, can you see…?"

There was dead silence in the room.

"Get it?" asked Earl. "It's like the national anthem." He sang it again. "Jose, can you see…"

"Right," said Reginald. "Well, I don't think we necessarily need to write *that* one down, but that's very good. Thank you, Earl. A very fine joke. Very well told, too."

"I think he needs to work on his timing," said Scoop.

"All right, now we're on a roll," said Reginald. "Now the creative juices are really going to start flowing. Who's next? Who has one?"

"Well," said the governor, "let's see if I can remember how this goes." He uncrossed his legs and sat forward on the couch. "Now mind you, I'm not very good at telling jokes. I told you that right up front."

"Yes, yes, Governor," said Reginald. "Please proceed."

"Well, it seems there was this colored fella," the governor began.

"Good, good," said Reginald eagerly. "That's perfect. That's exactly what we need. Keep going."

"And this colored fella…well, it seems he owned a pickup truck," continued the governor.

"Right," said Reginald. "Good."

"And one day he's loading up this here pickup truck with garbage," said the governor.

"Good, good," said Reginald. "What kind of garbage?"

"What?"

"What kind of garbage is he loading the pickup truck with?" asked Reginald.

"How the hell do I know?" said the governor. "It doesn't make any goddamn difference! That ain't part of the joke! Now will you clam up?"

"Absolutely," said Reginald. "Please, go ahead. You're doing marvelously, Governor."

"Marvelously," said Bret.

"Well this colored fella gets done loading up the truck and he realizes he doesn't have anything to tie down the load with. So he climbs up into the bed of the truck and lays down on top of all the garbage to keep it from falling off. Okay, so later on the truck is going down the highway and this colored fella is laying on top of everything in the back…"

Scoop looked up, perplexed. "Who's driving?"

"What?"

"Who's driving the truck?" asked Scoop. "I mean, if he's lying in the back holding the load down, who's—"

"I don't goddamn know who's driving!" shot the governor. "It doesn't make any goddamn difference! His brother. His Aunt Petunia. Who the hell cares?"

"Maybe the truck was stolen," suggested Earl. "Is that it, Governor? Was the truck stolen?"

"No, the truck wasn't stolen, you little pipsqueak! Now will all of you just shut the hell up and let me tell it?"

"Absolutely," said Reginald. "Everybody please be quiet so the governor can finish. Go ahead, Governor. You're doing wonderfully. So this black gentleman is driving down the road with his Aunt Petunia. Then what?"

"*It's not his*—" The governor suppressed his rage. "It's *not* his Aunt Petunia," he said in measured tones. "It's just…*someone*. Someone else is driving the truck, okay? It doesn't make any difference who it is. Okay?"

"Okay," said Reginald. "Then what?"

"Well," the governor continued, "it seems there's this other fella standing by the side of the road and the pickup truck goes by with the colored fella riding in back. And this guy by the side of the road, he says…he says…" There was a long moment while the governor's face displayed a succession of amusement, concentration and, ultimately, befuddlement.

"Goddamn, I can't remember," said the governor.

"I don't get it," said Earl. "Why is that supposed to be funny?"

"It's *not* supposed to be funny!" said the governor. "I don't remember the goddamn punch line! All right? I *told* you that right up front. I *told* you I was no goddamn good at this."

"Nonsense, Governor," said Reginald. "It was a wonderful joke. Wasn't it, Bret?"

"Wonderful," said Bret. "Do you know any others, Governor?"

"I still don't get it," Earl whispered to Scoop. Suddenly his face lit up. "Oh, I know a really sick one!"

"Good, now we're on a roll," said Reginald. "Tell us."

"What turns blue and goes round and round?" said Earl. "A midget in a washing machine."

Scoop nodded. "Yeah, I'd say that's fairly sick."

"Excellent, Earl," said Reginald. "Not exactly what we're looking for, but excellent nonetheless."

"Why isn't it what we're looking for?" Earl protested. "What's wrong with it?"

Reginald smiled gently. "It's not that there's anything *wrong* with it per se, Earl. It's just that…well, exactly who's going to be offended by it? Midgets? I mean, I hardly think it makes that much difference if we lose the midget vote."

"Midgets don't vote," said Scoop. "They can't reach the levers in the booth."

The governor suddenly brightened. "Hey, I know. What do you call a Jew with hemorrhoids?"

"Excellent!" said Reginald. "That's perfect, Governor. That's just the sort of stuff we need. All right, I'll bite. What *do* you call a Jew with hemorrhoids?"

The governor's face went blank. "Damn… I can't seem to remember that one, either. Goddamn it, I *told* you I was no good at this. Told you that right up front."

"Oh for Christ's sake," said Scoop. "Look, why don't we just write our own? Wouldn't that be easier than trying to remember one?"

"Could we do that?" asked Earl.

"Why the hell not?" said Scoop. "Where do you think jokes come from, anyway? Someone just makes them up. It's not like you need a doctorate in English or anything."

"An inspired suggestion, Scoop," said Reginald. "Uh…why don't you start us off?"

"Okay," said Scoop. "Uh…let's see. Um...okay, here goes… A prostitute walks into a bar." He wrote it on his yellow legal pad.

"I like it, I like it," said Reginald. "It's fairly pregnant with possibility. Only…how about making her black?"

"How about making her a Jew?" suggested Bret.

"Hey, why not make her a dyke?" said the governor, chuckling. "I really like a good dyke joke."

"Okay, okay," said Scoop, scribbling madly.

"Read that back to us," said Reginald.

"A black Jewish lesbian prostitute walks into a bar," said Scoop.

"I still don't see what's wrong with my midget joke," said Earl.

"Will you forget about the damn midget joke!" Reginald snapped. He closed his eyes and took several deep breaths. "I'm sorry, Earl. I yelled at you and that was counterproductive. Your midget joke was wonderful. Really, quite delightful. Wasn't it everyone?"

"Best midget joke I've heard in years," said Scoop.

"We all loved the midget joke," Reginald continued. "It's just that we're aspiring to offend a slightly larger segment of the population, that's all. You know, women, minorities, homosexuals…"

"How about the handicapped?" suggested the governor.

Reginald's eyes brightened. "The handicapped! Of course! That's brilliant, Governor. Even people who aren't handicapped are offended by jokes that ridicule the disabled." Then, more cautiously, "Uh…do you actually *know* any handicapped jokes, Governor?"

The governor thought for a moment. "As a matter of fact, I reckon I do. Let's see now…seems there was this fella with no legs who was wheeling himself down the street. And, uh…he meets, uh… a lady with a dog. Yeah, that's it. And the guy asks 'Does your dog bite?' and she says 'no,' see? And he goes to pet the dog and what do you know but the mutt up and bites him. So the fella goes 'I thought you said your dog didn't bite.' And the lady says…she says…" The governor began rocking back and forth on the couch, his face pinched up with laughter. "…she says 'That's not my dog.' Get it? 'That's not *my dog*!' The governor was laughing so hard now that tears were filling his eyes. "Goddamn it," he gasped between chuckles. "I did it! I remembered the goddamn punch line!"

"Governor," said Reginald, "what does that have to do with the man not having any legs?"

"Eh?" said the governor, wiping the moisture from his eyes. "What?"

"The joke was supposed to be about the handicapped," said Reginald, "but the fact that he hasn't any legs is wholly irrelevant to the punch line."

"Oh." The governor's laughter subsided and his face turned suddenly serious. "Crap, I think that's the wrong joke. Well, I told you I was no damn good at this."

"Told us that right up front," confirmed Scoop.

"All right, never mind," said Reginald, trying hard not to appear frustrated. "Let's stick with Scoop's idea. Uh…Scoop, what do we have so far?"

Scoop glanced down at the legal pad in his lap. "A black Jewish lesbian prostitute walks into a bar," he read.

"All right," said Reginald, "that's an excellent start. What next?"

Nobody in the circle said anything.

"Come on, gentlemen," Reginald pleaded. "We can handle this. It isn't that difficult. Just use your imaginations. Imagine that you're a black Jewish lesbian prostitute and you've just walked into a bar. All right? Now, what would be the first thing you'd do?"

"Order a drink?" suggested Scoop.

"Good," said Reginald. "Write it down."

Earl brightened. "Hey, wait a minute. I know some Polish jokes. How can you tell a Polish submarine? It's got screen windows."

"I really do admire your persistence on this, Earl," said Reginald in a tone of voice that made it clear just the opposite was true. "But really, Polish jokes are so…*passé*, don't you think? I mean, nobody's really all that offended by Polish jokes."

Earl fairly pouted. "I'll bet *Poles* are."

"Hey, I got one!" the governor said excitedly. "Remember the punch line and everything. Listen. It's a…a…oh, yeah. How do you fit four faggots in a crowded bar? Turn one of the barstools upside down!"

Earl furrowed his brow. "I don't get it."

"You don't get what?" asked Scoop.

"I don't get the joke. How is turning a barstool over going to help them fit in the bar? Does it take up less room that way or something?"

"No, it's not the amount of room the *barstool* takes up," said Scoop. "That's got nothing to do with it. It's just...you know. They're *gay*."

"Yes," said Earl, clearly still not getting it.

"And when you turn a barstool over, it's got...you know, legs. It's got four legs," said Scoop.

"Uh huh," said Earl.

"Allow me, Scoop," Reginald interrupted. "Earl, the joke is referring to certain sexual practices of the homosexual male. The implication is that the legs of the overturned barstool will serve in a phallic capacity. It's a reference to the homosexual tendency towards anal delectation."

Earl looked more confused than ever. "What do you mean... *delectation*?"

"Oh, for Christ's sake," said the governor, leaning forward. "Look, when a barstool is right side up, you can only seat one of them. When it's upside down, you can seat all *four* of them. They're gonna sit down and put the legs of the barstool up their *asses*! Get it?"

"Oh," said Earl, although it was clear the governor's words still hadn't quite sunk in. And then, a moment later, Earl's eyes suddenly widened. "*Oh*! I get it!"

"Praise the fucking lord," said the governor. "Hallelujah." He turned to face Reginald. "So what do you think, boy? Do we go with my joke or not?"

Reginald considered the question. "I believe it to be appropriately offensive. However, it will primarily offend the gay community, most of whose members wouldn't have been expected to vote for you anyway. No, I'm afraid it just won't push enough buttons for enough mainstream voters. I believe we should follow Scoop's suggestion and focus our energies on creating our own joke, tailor-made for our own particular requirements. Uh...Scoop, read back what we have so far."

"A black Jewish lesbian prostitute walks into a bar," said Scoop. He glanced down at his notes. "She orders a drink," he added.

The meeting continued through the rest of the morning until, by that afternoon, the campaign staff had finally completed what they believed to be the ultimate in tasteless humor, a joke that was so vulgar and disgusting it was guaranteed to offend absolutely everyone.

And it was that very evening that the governor, with no small amount of glee, moved to put the plan into action. After the completion of yet another campaign rally, during which he had delivered The Speech for what surely must have been the thousandth time, the governor found himself surrounded, as usual, by a bevy of reporters, all firing questions at him on a variety of topics and eagerly scribbling down whatever vague generalities he issued in reply.

"Say, boys," said the governor, unable to suppress a grin, "y'all want to hear a joke?"

When the reporters all readily consented, the governor cleared his throat, hitched up his polyester pants, dug his hands deep into his pockets, and began.

"Well sir, it seems this black Jewish lesbian prostitute walks into a bar. And she walks right on up to the bartender and orders a drink, see?" The governor began chuckling, his heavy frame shaking like an overloaded washing machine on the spin cycle. "So she says 'Let me have a screwdriver.' And the bartender...the bartender says..." The governor was chuckling so hard now that there was moisture in his eyes. "...he says 'Straight up or on the rocks?' And the hooker...the hooker says.."

All at once, the governor's face went blank. "Uh...she says... she says...uh, 'if you turn one of these barstools over, you'd be able to fit more midgets in here.' No, damn, that's not right. How the hell does it go again? She says...she says 'If you had hemorrhoids and no legs, you'd better be careful where you sit.' No, shit, that ain't it..." The governor began sweating profusely.

"Are you all right, Governor?" asked one of the reporters. "Would you like to sit down?"

"How...how do you tell a Jewish pickup truck?" stammered the governor, his eyes wild with confusion. "It's got screen windows. No, crap! That doesn't make any sense!" The governor's face was covered with sweat now and he swayed unsteadily on his feet.

"Someone get the governor a glass of water!" shouted one of the reporters.

"Give him air! Give him air!" shouted another.

"It's not my dog!" the governor sputtered. "She says 'It's not my dog!'"

"Pardon me, gentlemen," said Reginald, elbowing his way through the throng of reporters, most of whom were standing dumbfounded with varying expressions of concern and alarm on their faces. "The governor clearly isn't feeling well. His schedule has been particularly grueling today. Please excuse us." Hastily, Reginald led the governor away by the arm.

They pushed their way through a crowd of cheering supporters, reporters shouting questions, cameras flashing.

"I told you I was no damn good at telling jokes," said the governor. "Told you that right up front. Now the media's going to think I'm some kind of goddamn fool."

"The media's not going to say a word about this, Governor," said Reginald. "Believe me, by tomorrow morning they're going to have far more important things to talk about. The Yeager campaign just went ballistic."

"What?"

"Just get in the car, Governor."

The governor climbed into the backseat of the rented car, where Scoop and Bret were already seated. Reginald got into the passenger side of the front seat, where Earl sat waiting behind the wheel. The car radio was switched on, cranked up to an all-news station. As soon as Reginald slammed the front door shut, Earl threw the car into drive.

"What's the latest?" Reginald asked.

"He just issued a statement denying everything," said Earl. "And he's calling a press conference for tomorrow morning."

"How the hell can he deny it?" Scoop asked no one in particular. "He was caught red-handed. Didn't they say they found the money on him?"

"What money?" asked the governor. "What's going on?"

"All in tens and twenties," said Earl. "Yeager is claiming it's not his briefcase."

"The press is going to find that difficult to believe," said Reginald, "considering it has his initials on it."

"His initials," repeated Bret.

"And what about the drugs?" asked Scoop. "I suppose he doesn't know anything about that either?"

"Drugs?" said the governor. "What drugs?"

"He claims the girls brought the drugs in with them," said Earl.

"Christ, this is too much," said Scoop, rubbing his brow. "Why the hell couldn't something like this have happened to us? Huh? Is that too much to ask for? We couldn't have invented something this good if we had spent a month planning it."

"Have they found out who the girls were yet?" asked Reginald.

"*What* girls?" the governor demanded. "Someone tell me what the hell happened!"

"They haven't released any of their names to the press," said Earl, "but they *have* notified the parents."

"Parents?" Scoop sounded surprised. "I didn't hear that. They were underage?"

"Worse," said Earl. "Girl Scouts. Every single one of them. Troup 357. Evidently someone told them if they went along with it they could earn a merit badge. In rope-tying, I think."

"And what did Yeager say?" asked Reginald.

"Claims he doesn't know any of them," said Earl. "Claims he doesn't know how they got into his hotel room or what they were doing with the cucumbers."

"And the crack pipe," Scoop added. "Claims that's not his either. Shit, this is too good. Why...? Why the hell couldn't it have been *us*?"

"Goddamn it all!" the governor shouted, his face red. "Someone tell me just what the hell is going on!"

"I'll tell you one thing," Scoop continued. "I don't care about the drugs, I don't care about the money, and I don't care about the girls. I don't even care how they all ended up in his hotel room. I just want to know one thing. How the hell did he get the sheep past the front desk without being noticed?"

9/ New York, April 19th

Within the week, Yeager had dropped out of the race, leaving only two candidates vying for the Democratic nomination— Ed Mondukis and Thurmond Stonewall.

Of course, Mondukis was rubbing elbows with the press as frequently as possible, trying to get as much media coverage as he could. He appeared on the cover of Newsweek smiling confidently. He appeared on prime time television, having an intimate chat with Katie Couric. He appeared at Shea Stadium, waving from the stands and wearing a Mets baseball cap during the first game of a double-header against Pittsburgh.

The governor, on the other hand, was staying shy of the press. For one thing, his campaign staff wanted to limit his exposure as much as possible, in hopes of losing the race. But perhaps more importantly, his staff feared that, if the press got too close to the campaign, they might somehow stumble upon the details of the scam. Of course, his staff also worried about the opposite danger: the very fact that the governor was limiting the press' access to him was starting to appear awfully suspicious, considering the fact that he was supposed to be trying to win votes. The campaign appeared to be in a bind.

Until Scoop concocted a solution. What if one reporter was given exclusive access to the governor? That way the campaign could still limit the governor's accessibility, but could use the terms of the exclusive agreement as a handy excuse to avoid other reporters. Naturally, the press would still have access to the governor during public appearances and there would still be the usual entourage of reporters following the governor's campaign wherever it went, some of them even traveling in the governor's own bus. But the governor would refuse to grant in-depth interviews to any of them.

Only one reporter would be able to get that close to him. If the strategy wouldn't completely eliminate the danger of discovery, it might at least limit it.

As to which reporter should be granted the highly coveted honor of sitting at the governor's right hand and transcribing his every uttered gem, there was no doubt in Scoop's mind. Sarah Roman was the obvious choice. First of all, she had clearly expressed her desire to be given just such access to the governor. And secondly, she represented a publication which Scoop considered pure fluff, a magazine that had never broken a significant hard news story since its glossy pages had first hit the newsstands. The chances of her uncovering any information about the real motive of the governor's campaign seemed, at best, remote. Scoop pitched the idea to the Worthingtons and they agreed.

But there was an ulterior motive to Scoop's recommendation of Sarah. In essence, Scoop wanted to assure that she would continue following the governor's campaign. Not that he was in any way sentimental about her, or so he told himself. He had just gotten used to her, that was all. He had just gotten used to her wisecracks and her half-smile and her brand of perfume and the way she tilted her head sometimes when she talked and the way she chewed the end of her pencil when deep in thought and the way she casually tossed the hair away from her face with the back of her hand when she laughed. That was all.

They had gotten in the habit of meeting fairly regularly, he and Sarah. At first they would just meet by accident in a bar and end up sharing a round of drinks. Then they started deliberately meeting for lunch. Now they were in the habit of breaking bread together almost every day. Nothing in the least romantic, to be sure—a couple of sandwiches wolfed down in Scoop's hotel room, some hot dogs grabbed from a passing pushcart on the way to one of the governor's rallies. Still, it had become something they both expected and, if the truth be known, Scoop had begun looking forward every day to their shared meal.

They talked about politics, mostly—what the polls were predicting, what the pundits were saying, what the mood of the voters seemed to be. Sometimes Sarah would try to pump him for information about the governor or the campaign's strategy. And sometimes, just to please her, he would invent tidbits of information to feed her. There were times when he almost felt she was using him, that the only reason she spent time with him was to try to glean information about the governor. But then there were times, when he manufactured such information for her, that he felt perhaps he was using her, too.

Through it all, Scoop felt as if there existed a tacit understanding between the two of them, an unspoken bond. In fact, in some ways Scoop almost felt as if Sarah were a mirror of himself. Sarah's training had been in journalism, as had his. They both played their cards close to their chests, never revealing more about themselves or their real motives than was absolutely necessary. But most of all, they were both well-versed in the intricacies of national politics and they both viewed the campaign through a lens of amusement and knowing cynicism. There were times when Scoop felt as if the entire political process was taking place on stage, and he and Sarah were the only two sitting in the audience, snickering derisively. They were the only people truly capable of appreciating the farce and the irony, the only ones who really "got" the joke.

Scoop sensed a change taking place in him since he had met Sarah. He had not seriously thought about being romantically involved with a woman in years, had not thought about marriage in close to a decade. But now, during long meetings when Bret would talk endlessly about campaign finances or Earl would drone on about the latest poll results, Scoop would find himself unexpectedly transported to worlds of domestic fantasy. Suddenly he was sitting in a modestly furnished living room, bouncing a small child on his knee, a child who giggled and shrieked and pleaded with him not to stop. He was mowing the lawn and clipping the weeds and trimming the hedges, complaining about having to perform such tasks while inwardly loving every moment of it. He was lying in bed, holding his wife close to him, feeling her heart beat and listening to the slow, steady rhythm of her breath. And it wasn't until he suddenly recognized his wife's face as Sarah's that he would abruptly snap out of his reverie.

Moreover, ever since he had met Sarah, Scoop was becoming more and more conscious of somehow being in pain. He was unable to locate the exact origin of the sensation, for it didn't appear to be physical in nature. Rather, it seemed to be deeper than that, a pain of the very soul. Further, Scoop somehow sensed that the pain was not new, that it had been there a very long time and that only now was he becoming aware of it. Beneath her mask of cynicism, Scoop felt sure that Sarah must be feeling the same pain and this only served to deepen his attraction towards her.

But if Scoop felt there were changes going on at some deep, barely perceived level inside him, it was the far more blatant changes in the governor's behavior that would demand the immediate attention of the campaign staff in the days ahead.

"I've had it!" the governor announced one afternoon.

Scoop, Reginald and the governor were standing in the backroom of the governor's New York campaign headquarters, located in downtown Manhattan, after the governor had just concluded another in a seemingly endless procession of campaign rallies. The office was identical to all the other headquarters they had hastily established along the campaign trail—a converted storefront, now filled to capacity with cheap, identical green desks and mismatched office chairs, the stuffing of the latter peeking through the upholstery, more often than not. All the desks were piled high with papers and manila folders and white Styrofoam cups half-filled with two-day old coffee and floating cigarette butts. Plywood walls had been thrown up to separate the office into several rooms, thereby conveying the illusion of privacy.

"Calm down, Governor," said Reginald, patting the air before him as if the very gesture might somehow decrease the governor's blood pressure. "There's nothing to get excited about. Whatever it is, we can handle it. Now just back up and tell me what's bothering you."

"I'm sick of it, goddamn sick of it!" fumed the governor. He paced back and forth across the small room, a scowl on his face, his shirt stained at the armpits. "If I have to make that same damn speech one more time, I'll puke. Up and puke, right there in front of the whole damn crowd."

"Hmm," said Scoop quietly. "Maybe not a bad idea."

"Shut up, wise guy," snapped the governor. "I'm damn serious about this. I mean, how many goddamn times have I read that speech already? Huh? A thousand? A million? And I still don't know what the hell it means. 'It is a time to rekindle the torch of freedom.' 'It is the dawning of a new age for America.' What is that shit?"

"Shh," cautioned Reginald. "Governor, please." He motioned toward one of the thin, plywood walls. "It's very easy for someone to hear..." Reginald stopped short. "What the hell am I saying? No, never mind, Governor. Shout all you want."

"You're damn right I'll shout all I want," said the governor. "And another thing. I'm sick and tired of you and your damn brother telling me what to do. I ain't no patsy, boy. You hear me? Sure as shit there's gonna be some changes around here. You mark my words, boy. Sure as shit." The governor stormed out of the room and slammed the door behind him, the flimsy walls trembling from the impact.

"What the hell's gotten into him?" asked Scoop.

Reginald slowly shook his head and sighed. "Some asinine pollster predicted that if the election were held today, the governor and Mondukis would finish in a dead heat. It just came over the radio a short while ago."

"What? That's ridiculous."

"Yes, yes, it's ridiculous," agreed Reginald. "But ever since our esteemed governor heard it, he's been impossible to deal with."

Scoop frowned. "What the hell is he thinking?"

"I have no idea. All I know is he keeps talking about wanting to take charge of the campaign, being his own man, all that sort of rubbish."

"Sounds like he's been reading his own headlines," observed Scoop. And then, in a lower voice, "You know, Reg, that might not be such a bad idea."

"Heh? What do you mean?"

"I mean turning the governor loose," said Scoop. "Look, we've tried everything else. Every time we've tried to blow up the campaign, it's backfired. Maybe we've been making this more difficult than it has to be. What if we just let the governor ad lib? Let him do the damage himself. I mean, listen to him. The man can't string two words together without tripping over his own tongue. He's a born loser, right? That's why you chose him in the first place, wasn't it? If we just took away his cue cards and his pre-written speeches, he'd self-destruct on the spot."

Slowly, a smile crept across Reginald's face. "Just let Stonewall be Stonewall," he said. "It does have a certain poetic irony, doesn't it? It's so simple, it just might work. All right, then. Let's do it."

So the governor was given the green light. His staff would still provide him with pre-written scripts and suggested answers to reporters' questions, but the governor was given complete freedom to deviate from those scripts whenever he so chose. From now on he was to speak his mind, such as it was.

The results were dramatic and instantaneous. That very evening, at a rally in Queens, the governor departed from a prepared statement about education to deliver a short, impromptu speech on a related subject.

"Listen," the governor said, straightening his tie and leaning forward towards the microphone, "let me tell you all something. Y'all want to know what the real problem is with the educational system in this country? 'Cause I'll tell you all what it is. It's these goddamn immigrants coming in across the border every day of the week, that's what. Coming in from Mexico, coming in from Haiti, coming in from Vietnam, coming in from who in God's name knows where. And they come to this country, unable to speak a lick of English, with nothing to show for themselves but the clothes on their back and a case of venereal disease. And they expect us to teach them the language and give them an education, just like that. Just expect it, without giving anything in return. And we bend over backwards to give it to them, too, that's the damn shame of it. Special ed classes, English as a second language courses—that's where your tax dollars are going. That's what's draining the educational system in this country."

The governor's comments were splashed across the front pages of all the next day's New York dailies. STONEWALL CRITICIZES BILINGUAL EDUCATION FOR RECENT IMMIGRANTS, SUGGESTS REFORM TO EDUCATION SYSTEM, REMARKS ENRAGE SOME IN IMMIGRANT COMMUNITY, CANDIDATE UNREPENTANT read the headline in The New York Times.

THURM SLAMS WETBACKS, read the headline in The Post.

The Times also ran an editorial strongly condemning the governor's remarks as xenophobic. But that did nothing to dissuade Stonewall. That afternoon, while answering a reporter's question on Israel, he launched another barb.

"Tell me something," he said, his brow furrowed with disgust. "What the hell are New York Jews so pushy about? I mean hell, they practically own the whole damn city. They've got more money than God himself. But you say one thing about Israel they don't like and they turn into a bunch of sniveling eight-year-olds. Gets me to thinking that maybe they're living in the wrong damn country."

When the story was reported on the evening news, Jewish groups were outraged. The Anti-Defamation League hurled charges of anti-Semitism at the governor and demanded an apology.

The governor was unfazed. The next day at a fund-raising luncheon in Brooklyn, he blasted the Americans with Disabilities Act.

"Does it make sense," he asked rhetorically, "for a business owner to have to redesign his whole damn store just so one guy in a wheelchair can fit through the door? I ask you. I mean, I know times sure are tough out there, but no one should have to put out that kind of money and effort, all on account of one goddamn customer. Hell, for that kind of money, you can hire someone to carry the sorry bastard through the damn door!"

The press couldn't crank out the headlines fast enough. The New York Post even coined an expression to describe the governor's more outrageous statements. It referred to them as "Stonewall stunners." Various organizations began staging demonstrations at the governor's campaign appearances, which served to increase his press coverage even more. The media was full of spokespeople from one group or another blasting the governor—blacks, Jews, Hispanics, the disabled. With just three days to go until the primary, Stonewall seemed fast on his way to becoming the most hated person in New York.

"You don't suppose he actually *believes* any of that crap, do you?" Scoop asked cautiously.

He and Reginald were sitting in a delicatessen on Delancy Street that was a particular favorite of Scoop's. Various meats and cheeses hung in the window like cold cut chandeliers and the air was permeated with the perfume of freshly cut corned beef.

"Hmm?" said Reginald. "What do you mean?"

"Stonewall. You don't think he really believes the things he's saying, do you?" Scoop took a bite of his pastrami on rye with mustard.

"Of course not," said Reginald, munching his turkey on whole wheat with mayo. "The good governor is doing precisely what he ought to be doing. Stirring up controversy. Infuriating the masses. Making a general nuisance of himself."

"Yeah, I guess. But he sure as hell seems to be getting a lot of press in the process."

"Yes, all of it negative," Reginald reminded him.

"Well, not all of it. What about the radio?"

"You don't mean the AM call-in shows?" said Reginald. "Scoop, don't be preposterous. The people who host those shows are professional cranks. They don't exert any real influence over public opinion. Just because Rush Limbaugh thinks the governor is God's gift to America doesn't mean the voters are going to follow suit."

Reginald put down his sandwich and studied Scoop's expression carefully. "Look, old boy, you're really not worried, are you? Everything's going marvelously, better than we possibly could have expected. The governor has managed to offend virtually every major special interest group in the state. We're down in the polls. We're getting the worst press we've gotten in months. Things are finally starting to look up. What on earth is bothering you?"

Scoop shook his head and examined the quickly rising bubbles of carbonation in his beer. "I don't know, Reg. Maybe it's just that things always seem to be going our way just before they blow up in our faces. I guess I'm just getting paranoid or something. Maybe I'd feel better if Mondukis were digging into the governor's background or running attack ads against him or something. I mean, why isn't he? We're the only rivals he's got left. Have you thought about that?"

"Attack ads? Why bother? The governor is self-destructing all on his own. The only attack ads Mondukis needs are the headlines." Reginald dabbed at his mouth with a napkin. "What's really bothering you, Scoop?"

"What do you mean?"

"Come on, I've known you too long. Now something is going on with you. What is it?"

Scoop turned to look out the window at the parade of pedestrians passing by on the sidewalk—women with baby carriages, teenage boys displaying gang colors, homeless men with shopping carts. "I don't know, Reg. Maybe I've just been doing this too damn long."

"Of course you have," said Reginald. "When was the last time you took a vacation? Not since I've known you. As soon as the campaign is concluded, I advise you to take a month off. No, two months. Go to the French Riviera. It's exquisite this time of year. I'll give you the names of all the best clubs and restaurants. Oh, and there's a four-star hotel there that's owned by a personal friend of mine. I'll give you his name, too. You'll be treated like absolute royalty. Mark my words. Given a modicum of rest and relaxation, you'll be back to your old self in no time."

"Yeah," said Scoop, still watching the street traffic. "I guess maybe you're right."

"Of course I am," said Reginald, picking up his sandwich again. "Trust me. There's absolutely nothing to worry about."

The following morning, the upcoming primary was forced off the front pages of the tabloids by a story that was considerably more sensational. Izzy Nauseous, lead singer for the thrash metal band Jane's In Chains, was convicted of raping a teenage girl in his hotel room during the band's last nationwide tour. The judge rejected the pleas of the council for the defense that Nauseous be allowed to serve his sentence by performing one hundred hours of community service and instead sentenced the rock superstar to ten years in prison. Nauseous was shown on television news reports being led away from the courthouse in handcuffs and dressed in a conservative blue suit instead of the black leather and chains with which he usually adorned himself. Shouting their support for the convicted man, crowds of teenagers in Jane's In Chains T-shirts had to be held back by police barricades as he was led to a police cruiser and driven away.

That afternoon, during a speech to the Albany Chamber of Commerce, the governor once again deviated from his prepared text to offer a personal perspective.

"If you all want to know what's wrong with the criminal justice system in this country, you don't have to look any further than Manhattan," said the governor. "You all see on the news that this here singer—or whatever the hell he is—is going to jail on account of having a good time with some groupie who probably wanted it just as much as he did? Well, never mind that. The point is they're sending this poor sap to jail for ten years. Now I ask you, what possible good is done for society by having this guy rot in jail? Hell, some of these rock stars have more money than the heads of major corporations. Why not give him a choice—go to jail or pay a million dollar fine?

We could sure use the money more than we could having to pay for the room and board of another convict."

To say that women's groups were outraged is an understatement. The president of the National Organization of Women blasted the governor's insensitivity and condemned him for suggesting that "someone should be able to buy his way out of prison so long as he has enough money."

But the press barely had time to react before the governor dropped another bombshell, that very evening when responding to a question about increased funding for AIDS research.

"I think it's a waste of money," the governor said. "I mean, I don't have anything against homosexuals. It isn't their fault they're the way they are. I just think instead of spending all this money trying to stamp out AIDS, maybe we'd be better off trying to stop what causes it in the first place. I don't know why some people are homosexual. I'm no scientist or anything. Seems to me, though, that if we were to redirect some of that AIDS research money towards trying to find out why some folks are homosexual in the first place, maybe we'd be able to find a cure for that. And then the whole AIDS problem would just go away. We could just let the gay folks who've already got it die off and your average decent citizens wouldn't have to worry about it anymore."

The American Medical Association immediately issued a disclaimer, explaining that homosexuality was not a disease and that the governor's comments had absolutely no basis in medical fact. That did little to appease gay rights groups, however, who announced an emergency rally to be held the following day in Times Square.

STONEWALL SUGGESTS HOMOSEXUALITY CAN BE CURED, DRAWS WRATH OF GAY RIGHTS ACTIVISTS, AMA DENIES GOVERNOR'S COMMENTS HAVE ANY LEGITIMACY, read the headline in The Times.

THURM SLAMS HOMOS, read the headline in The Post.

The evening before the New York primary, Scoop met Sarah for dinner at a small Thai restaurant on the Upper East Side of the city. Scoop had been getting even less sleep than usual and there were heavy bags beneath each of his eyes.

"God, you really look like shit," said Sarah.

"Thanks for saying so." He took a long drink of his Dewar's on the rocks. "It's been a hell of a week."

"I guess." Sarah sipped her margarita, a drink which Scoop had advised her against getting, reminding her that a Thai restaurant was probably not the best place to order one. Stubbornly, she had insisted on it and was now pretending it was the best drink she'd ever had, even though Scoop guessed it probably tasted like crap.

"The governor certainly seems to be drawing a lot of attention to himself these days," Sarah continued after a pause. "What the hell is going on? Can't get him to stick to the script anymore?"

Scoop forced a smile. "He's his own man. Hasn't he told you that enough times since you've started interviewing him?"

"Sure," said Sarah, "but you must realize how much his gaffes are hurting the campaign."

Absently, Scoop began rearranging his silverware into various geometric patterns. "Well, it is *his* campaign, after all. Besides, we've issued corrections after some of his more embarrassing misstatements. It happens in every campaign."

"A lame attempt at spin control if I ever saw one," said Sarah, lighting a cigarette. "Sometimes it seems as if you guys don't even want to win."

Scoop looked up sharply. "What do you mean? Of course we want to win. Why would you say something like that?"

"I don't know," said Sarah. "It's just that as I've looked into the history of the campaign, it seems as if some strange decisions have been made along the way. Like around spending money, for example."

Scoop felt a sensation like his stomach wall closing in on itself. "What about spending money?"

"Well, you've really been running the campaign on a shoestring, from what I can see. You've done next to no television advertising. Ever since the primaries started, you've only been hitting the major cities. I keep wondering what the hell you're waiting for."

Scoop looked down at the table, at his drink, across the room, everywhere but at Sarah. "Maybe we're just managing our budget better than most campaigns. There's no advantage to spending more money than you have to. We're still winning, aren't we?"

"You're coming in *second*," Sarah reminded him. "You're still behind Mondukis in the polls and getting lower every day with all the things the governor's been saying. I just don't get it. It's like the campaign is slipping away from you and you don't even care. Where's the big advertising blitz? Where's the big PR effort? Why are you guys holding back?"

Scoop glanced in her direction and suddenly, inadvertently, met her eyes. For a moment he thought he might blurt out the truth, just spill the whole thing out, right there over the plates of pad thai and chicken curry. He hated lying to her and somehow the whole ridiculous scheme was starting to seem less and less important to him now.

"Sarah...I..."

"Yes?" she asked, taking a deep drag on her cigarette.

Scoop found himself unable to maintain eye contact. He stared down at the food on his plate, lying half-eaten and suddenly not the slightest bit appetizing.

"I think maybe I should...I mean, I'm not sure..."

"What are you mumbling about?" asked Sarah.

"It's just that...."

"Is everything all right here?" a waiter interrupted. "Can I get you another beer, sir?"

"No," said Scoop. "No, everything's fine."

"You were saying?" prompted Sarah after the waiter had wandered off.

Scoop shook his head. "No, never mind. Look, what can I tell you? The governor has already gone further than any of the pundits predicted he would. Why argue with success? You and I both know how unpredictable the voters are. You can spend millions on TV commercials, you can inundate the whole fucking market, and the voter still ends up picking the other candidate because the other guy reminds him of his Uncle Harry or some damn thing. If we've been able to get as far as we have spending our money the way we have, I'd say that's pretty damn good."

"Okay, okay, keep your pants on." She flicked her cigarette in the ashtray and tossed her hair back with a quick jerk of her neck. "I just think it's curious, that's all."

* * *

I just think it's curious, that's all. The words echoed in Scoop's mind the rest of the night and throughout the next day, the day of the New York primary. They echoed in his mind while the governor was making his final campaign stops around the state and as the early returns began coming in from the polls. They continued echoing in his mind when the polls closed and the final results were tabulated, revealing that the governor had beaten Mondukis by a narrow margin of three percentage points.

Scoop knew that the press and the pollsters and the pundits would spend the next several days scrambling to explain the governor's unexpected victory. They would bandy about phrases like "disaffected voters" and "populist image" and even "conservative backlash." But personally, Scoop found that he wasn't all that surprised by the outcome of the election. In fact, there almost seemed to be a certain inevitability to it, as if the result would have been the same no matter what the governor or anyone else in the campaign had said or done. Boarding the bus for Philadelphia late that night, his eyes bleary from lack of sleep and the last cold snap of winter still clinging to the air. Scoop had the inexplicable feeling that the outcome of the entire race was completely out of everyone's hands and that he was merely a minor player in a history that had already been written.

On the bus, the governor sat in the seat next to Scoop. Scoop observed that the governor appeared to be in good spirits—smiling graciously, laughing and joking with the press, and generally carrying on like the laid-back son of Texas the American public was growing to know and love. After everyone had settled into their respective seats and the bus had lurched forward, beginning its brief journey southwest through the darkness of New Jersey, Scoop turned to face him.

"You seem pretty cheery," said Scoop.

"Yep," shrugged the governor. "I reckon so."

Scoop leaned forward and whispered in a voice that was barely audible. "You *do* know we were supposed to lose, don't you?"

The governor offered him a devious smile, the proverbial cat that had eaten the canary. "Of course I do, son," he whispered. "What kind of fool do you take me for?"

They rode without speaking for several minutes. Scoop felt himself being lulled gently towards sleep by the rhythmic sound of rubber on cement and the glare of streetlights that flashed by with hypnotic regularity. Beside him, Scoop sensed the governor shifting into a more comfortable position, then the sound of the man's breathing becoming shallower, more consistent. Scoop closed his eyes and let loose an exhausted sigh.

The sound came gently, quieter than Scoop had ever heard it before, barely audible above the din of the engine, almost as if the governor were talking in his sleep. Scoop might not have even recognized it as the governor's voice had he not been sure of its source, had the man not been sitting mere inches away from him.

"Nobody tells me," he murmured. "Nobody tells Thurmond Stonewall what to do. He's his own man. That's what they say. His own goddamn man. Speaks his mind, shoots from the hip. Look out, pardner. Shoot your damn head off. Hah. Hog tie ya and leave ya to bake in the sun. Hang ya and leave ya twisting in the wind. Hah. Goddamn bastards. Every one of them. Just two kinds of people, them that see and them that gotta be shown. Them that don't see just gotta be shown. That's all. Just two kinds.

"Thanks for cleaning up the town, marshal. Thanks for cleaning up the town. Town ain't big enough for the both of us. Hah. Fucking bastards. Tie your legs to two different horses and send them off in opposite directions. Burn your eyes out with a red hot poker. Fucking bastards. Somebody's gotta show them. Somebody's gotta show them. Gotta be shown. You know what I'm saying? Huh? You know what I'm saying? Sure you do. Sure you do…" The governor's voice trailed off and moments later the sound of his light snoring was intermingled with the roar of the motor.

Scoop didn't sleep the rest of the trip, just sat quietly, motionless, his eyes wide open, staring straight ahead into the darkness.

10/ Pennsylvania, April 26th

As soon as Reginald got the call, he convened an emergency meeting in his hotel room.

"Gentlemen, I have excellent news," he said, the orange blossom scent of his herbal tea perfuming the air. "Not twenty minutes ago, I received a call from none other than Felix Greene, Chairman of the Democratic National Committee. Mr. Greene requested a meeting with me for this very afternoon and, in response, I immediately cleared my schedule in order to accommodate him. The fact that Mr. Greene has made this request inevitably leads me to a singular conclusion."

"He's going to ask us to step aside," said Scoop, slurping black coffee from a white Styrofoam cup.

"Step aside?" said the governor. "How the hell do you know that?"

Reginald smiled condescendingly. "My good man, there's really no other viable explanation. Why else would Mr. Greene be requesting such a meeting? Ed Mondukis is clearly the leading candidate as well as the choice of the party elite. Mr. Greene is obviously going to ask us to step aside in the name of party unity. And we, of course, will comply forthwith."

"Thank God," said Scoop. "Just what we've been waiting for, an excuse to drop out of the race without it looking suspicious."

"Never mind eluding suspicion," said Reginald. "We're going to appear downright *noble*. We leak Mr. Greene's request to the press and everyone in the country will know that Thurmond Stonewall dropped out of the race, not because he wasn't equal to the competition, but because his own party came to him on bended knee and beseeched him to do so. And he, gracious and conscientious statesman that he is, made the ultimate sacrifice in the name of his party. Could anything be more selfless?"

"More selfless," said Bret.

"Hmph," snorted the governor and turned to look out the hotel window at the streets of Philadelphia eight stories below.

"Is there something wrong, Governor?" Reginald asked. "Something troubling you?"

"No," said the governor shortly. "Nothing. I'm...I'm just not so sure that's what this Greene fella wants to meet about, that's all."

"Why of course it is," said Reginald. "What other possible reason could there be? Trust me, Governor. There's absolutely nothing to worry about. This whole ordeal will be over soon."

The governor avoided Reginald's eyes. "Yeah. Yeah, I reckon so."

Scoop studied the governor—the way his arms dangled limply at his sides, the mild disgruntlement displayed on his face—and tried to guess what was going on in his mind. Ever since the night they had sat next to each other during the bus ride to Philadelphia, the night the governor had demonstrated such inexplicably bizarre behavior, Scoop had been keeping a careful eye on him. Not that Scoop even knew precisely what he was watching for. Some sign of further eccentricity perhaps? Was he expecting the governor to suddenly drop to all fours and start barking like a dog, right there in the middle of Reginald's hotel room? Or was he looking for a sign that the governor had just been pulling his leg that night on the bus? At any moment, Scoop half-expected the governor to wink at him from across the room and say "Had you going there for a minute, didn't I? Pulled one over on you, boy. Yessiree."

Of course now, drinking coffee in the clarity of daylight, the notion that the governor might not be completely right in the head seemed outlandish. After all, there he was, sitting and talking like any rational human being. Was there really any legitimate reason for Scoop to doubt his sanity? So the man talks to himself. Was that a crime? Was that grounds for being institutionalized? Besides, maybe he had just been talking in his sleep that night. Maybe. There were even moments when Scoop doubted that the occurrence had ever taken place. After all, it had been late, Scoop had been tired, the roar of the bus's engine had made it difficult to hear anything clearly. Perhaps Scoop had been the one who was dreaming, who had concocted the entire incident in his slumber. Now, sober and fully awake, Scoop found it hard to be sure.

Scoop had noticed only one other thing about the governor's behavior that seemed in any way suspicious. He had noticed it later that night, disembarking from the bus when they had reached their hotel in downtown Philadelphia. In the chill half-light of impending dawn, Scoop saw the governor carrying into the lobby a large brown satchel, tattered and faded with age. He probably wouldn't have noticed it but for the fact that the episode with the governor on the bus had been so strange, that the satchel did not appear to match any of the governor's other luggage, and that when a bellboy from the hotel offered to carry the satchel to the governor's room along with the rest of his belongings, the governor most steadfastly refused the offer. Scoop observed that the governor did not release the bag from his grip until sometime after he was in his own room, across the hall from Scoop's, and the door had swung shut. Scoop had been in the governor's room several times since then and had not noticed the satchel, either stacked in the corner with the rest of the governor's luggage or anywhere else in the room.

It had been a hectic few days since then. The governor had inadvertently snagged some more headlines when a New York AM radio station had offered him his own call-in talk show, should his presidential aspirations prove fruitless. The governor had joked with the press when asked about it, explaining that while he was certainly flattered by the offer he had other ambitions at the moment. In all the commotion, any concerns about the governor had receded into the back of Scoop's mind. But now, sitting in Reginald's hotel room, he found himself examining the governor's every motion—the way he crossed his legs and sipped his coffee.

"Well then," said Reginald, placing his tea on the coffee table with a grand, exaggerated gesture, as if to signal the meeting's conclusion like a judge banging a gavel. "I suggest we reconvene later this afternoon, after my conference with the good Mr. Greene. I am extremely optimistic that I will have auspicious news to report. Scoop, I trust you will be available to join me at this meeting?"

"No prob," said Scoop, draining his coffee.

So, several hours later, Reginald and Scoop met Felix Greene, Chairman of the Democratic National Committee, in the hotel's modest restaurant. Greene turned out to be a tall, soft-spoken man with wire-rim glasses and a perpetually pained expression, as if he were in need of emergency dental work. He and Reginald both ordered lunch. Scoop ordered a Dewey.

"You're probably wondering why I asked for this meeting," said Greene, spreading an orange cloth napkin across his lap as the food was being brought to the table, "so I'll get right to the point."

"I must say you certainly have piqued our interest," Reginald replied. "Please do proceed."

"Well, to put it bluntly," said Greene, "there are only two men left standing—your man and Ed Mondukis."

Reginald cut himself a piece of bluefish. "Yes, we certainly seem to have frustrated the predictions of some of our detractors."

"To be sure," said Greene. "No offense intended, but there were plenty of people in the party who didn't think Stonewall would make it out of New Hampshire."

Reginald smiled sheepishly, as if embarrassed by the campaign's unexpected success. "No offense taken. We're all friends here."

"And many of us have been very impressed with the kind of numbers you've been racking up during the primaries," continued Greene.

"As well you should be, sir," said Reginald, returning his attention to his meal. "They're impressive numbers."

And an equally impressive performance, thought Scoop, exactly midway between graciousness and cockiness. Reginald was doing okay, playing his cards carefully.

"Still," said Greene, casually twirling some linguine around his fork, "at this point in the campaign, you must be questioning the wisdom of continuing."

Reginald's eyes shot up as if surprised. "I beg your pardon?"

"Well, I mean, the possibility must have at least crossed your mind," said Greene. "After all, Mondukis is leading in every major poll. He's already got almost enough electoral votes to take the convention on the first round. I don't...I don't know how else to say it." Greene looked at Reginald directly. "You do know you haven't got a chance of winning, don't you?"

Reginald feigned indignation as if he were angling for an Oscar nomination. "Mr. Greene, as you've been so candid as to freely acknowledge, the party has so far been wrong about my candidate's chances of success. What makes you think your predictions are any less fallacious now? I submit to you, sir, that the prospects of either candidate are uncertain until the campaign has reached its conclusion."

Greene held up his hand like a traffic cop trying to slow down a speeding motorist. "Now hold on there a minute, Reg. Don't get me wrong. Hear me out on this. All I'm saying is that the possibility must have at least crossed your mind. Hasn't it? For God's sake, you boys have done an incredible job. Everyone I talk to in the party is impressed. Your future couldn't be brighter, I can tell you that right now. The fact is, you've held in there longer than anyone predicted. But you've got a small staff—smaller than any of the other campaigns. All your people must be exhausted. And financially speaking, you boys must be running on fumes by now." Greene leaned back in his chair and sighed. "Now tell me honestly. Haven't you at least considered the possibility of dropping out?"

Reginald lowered his eyes. "Well, to be perfectly candid...yes, of course, the thought has crossed our minds..."

Greene smiled like a kindly father. "Of course it has. I knew it. It's only natural. That's why I came here today. That's why I had to meet with you. Because there's something I need to ask of you. Something that's a great personal sacrifice, to be sure, but something that's absolutely essential for the good of the party. Believe me, if there were any other way, I wouldn't be asking this. But promise me you'll at least think about it before you answer."

"I promise," said Reginald solemnly. "Go ahead."

"I...I need to ask you to make sure the governor stays in the race," said Greene.

"Well, I hardly know what to s—" Reginald stopped short. "What did you say?"

"I said I want you to promise me that the governor will *stay* in the race."

Scoop had never seen anything like it, certainly not from someone so typically unflappable as Reginald. In the course of the next several seconds, Reginald's face registered a rapid succession of emotions ranging from disbelief to anger to confusion and back to disbelief. It was as if his face had suddenly turned to Silly Putty and was being stretched into a multitude of minute variations.

"I know what a hardship this must be to you," Greene continued, "after all the work you've done already. Running a presidential campaign isn't easy, particularly when you know you're backing a losing cause. Believe me, I don't feel good about having to ask you this. But you must believe me when I tell you that it's absolutely crucial."

"I…I don't understand," Reginald managed to stammer, his eyes glazed over.

"It's pretty simple, really," said Greene. "I'm sure you've noticed that the president has been grabbing most of the headlines lately. He just signed that new agreement with Russia. He's got the economic summit in Western Europe coming up next week. He's getting the best press he's gotten since he took office. The fact is, the only thing that's keeping Mondukis on the front pages at all is Stonewall. As long as Stonewall's still in the race, the contest between them is still news. Once he drops out and Mondukis' nomination is assured, the press stops paying attention. Mondukis will be lucky to get a mention on the society page between now and the convention."

Greene wiped his mouth with his orange napkin. "That's why it's so important for Stonewall to stay in the race. Without him, Mondukis goes into journalism limbo for the next three months and the president has a field day. Besides, you know as well as I do that your candidate has been saying some pretty outlandish things lately. To most voters, that makes Mondukis look awfully reasonable by comparison, which is just fine with us."

Reginald cleared his throat, the color finally beginning to come back into his face. "I…I hardly know what to say."

"Just say you'll think about it, that's all," said Greene.

"Certainly," Reginald said unsteadily. "Certainly we will."

"Good," said Greene. He finished off the last of his linguine and put down his fork. "Oh, by the way, I've heard that the Mondukis people have been offering to set up a debate and that the governor has been resisting. We'd really like to see that debate take place. It would be great publicity. Might even knock the president out of the spotlight for a day or two. Besides, your man is running second. He's got nothing to lose."

"We'll take that under advisement," said Reginald mechanically, still dazed.

Greene smiled and turned towards Scoop. "You've been awfully quiet through all of this, Joel. What do you think?"

Scoop shrugged. "I think I'll have another scotch."

The Stonewall camp had been ducking Mondukis' offers to debate in hopes that the press might start criticizing the governor on the issue. Now there seemed to be little choice but to rise to the challenge and accept.

Of course, when Reginald finally regained his senses, he immediately devised a way in which the debate could be used to their advantage. The governor was going to do the debate cold—no scripts, no notes, no prepared answers. The staff wasn't even going to rehearse the governor, as was the usual practice of candidates before a major political debate. The governor was going to be working without a net.

The debate was set for just two days before the Pennsylvania primary. There would be a live audience and a single moderator—television talk show host Phil Riviera. Riviera hosted a daytime program out of Philadelphia that regularly dealt with topics ranging from fashion to incest to adultery and included interviews with a widely diverse cross-section of people, from women who had been molested by space aliens to children who were raised by Satanists. Throughout the campaign, however, Riviera had been making a concerted bid for legitimacy by booking several political analysts on the show and discussing some considerably more far-reaching topics. As a result, he was finally being given the opportunity he had long been seeking—the chance to moderate a debate between two presidential candidates, thereby solidifying his image as a serious journalist.

On the night of the debate, the television studio at Philadelphia's station WRVP was packed with a jumble of spectators and electronic equipment. There were almost twice as many cameras as were usually there for a broadcast and the foreground of the stage was littered with a criss-crossing network of cables and wires. The press had laid claim to the first several rows of seats, but further back was seated a large and restless studio audience. Riviera thought he hadn't seen such an excited crowd since the last time he had featured exotic male dancers on his show.

"Hello Philadelphia and hello America," Riviera began the broadcast. He had the booming voice of an announcer from ESPN, but his smile was strictly Home Shopping Network. His thick, white hair contrasted sharply with the dark tan of his complexion and, with his bushy moustache and eyebrows, he resembled nothing so much as a silver-haired Mussolini.

"Tonight, the two remaining Democratic candidates for president meet each other for their first one-on-one debate—Senator Ed Mondukis of Maine and Governor Thurmond Stonewall of Texas. I'm Phil Riviera and I'll be the moderator for tonight's debate. We'll begin with a question for Senator Mondukis. Senator, if you are elected president, what will you do to revitalize the nation's economy?"

Mondukis answered in a solemn tone, his gaze directed at neither Riviera nor the audience, but at the nearest television camera. "First of all, I want to point out that it's very difficult to separate all the factors that influence our national economy. They're all interconnected and we can't just tinker with one of them and hope to immediately fix the problem. We need to take the long view, take all the related factors into consideration, make constructive changes carefully, and then give them enough time to have the desired effect. But most of all, we must all be prepared to make sacrifices—equal sacrifices across the board for every American. Because the simple truth is it's going to take a lot of hard work and sacrifice to turn this economy around, but I'm convinced that it *can* be done. Now I've put together a five-point plan to reduce the federal budget deficit, which I believe will steer the country in the right direction. First of all—"

"Sorry, Senator," interrupted Riviera, "but I'm afraid your time is up. Governor Stonewall, would you care to respond?"

The governor grinned and squinted past the television lights to the studio audience. "Howdy, folks. My name's Stonewall and I'm the other guy." There was an appreciative chuckle from the audience. "First of all, let me say what a genuine thrill it is for me to be here in the City of Brotherly Love. You know, a lot of people make jokes about Philadelphia, but as far as I'm concerned that's just a load of bull jerky. I've had the pleasure of staying in this fair city a number of times over the years and I've always been impressed by your cleanliness and grateful for your hospitality." The crowd applauded loudly in response.

"Now, turning to the remarks of my opponent here," the governor continued, gesturing towards Mondukis with a casual jerk of the head, "all I can say is—jumpin' saddle sores, Ed, lighten up a little, will you? I haven't heard so many calls for sacrifices since the last time the Phillies had two men on and no out." The audience roared with laughter. "My opponent here seems to think that everything is doom and gloom. Well don't you believe him. America didn't become the greatest nation in the history of the world by fretting over our problems. We did it by holding our heads high, by being proud of our heritage, and by having faith in our dreams. Don't you let anyone— Senator Mondukis or anyone else—tell you to be ashamed of being an American."

"Now hold on, Governor," protested Mondukis, "I never said a damn thing about—"

"Sorry, Senator, it isn't your turn," Riviera interrupted. He flipped to the next in his stack of 3x5 index cards. "The next question is for Governor Stonewall. Governor, race has become a hot topic during this campaign. A recent study has shown there is still a big difference in the standards of living between whites and African-Americans. Some people have said that you, Governor, are not sensitive to the plight of minorities. How do you respond?"

The governor's expression turned suddenly serious. He cleared his throat and looked down at the podium before him as if holding back emotion. "You know, it really hurts me when people misinterpret some of the things I've said. The press has misquoted me, they've quoted me out of context—it's enough to make me cut back on talking to reporters, which is exactly what I've had to do. So let me take the opportunity to clear this thing up once and for all. I believe, and have always believed, that all men are created equal. I believe that every American, regardless of his race, creed or color, deserves the same educational opportunities and the same protection under the law. I believe that everyone has an equal right to work and live in this great land of ours. That's what I believe and I don't care who knows it."

"Senator Mondukis?" Riviera prompted.

The senator put down the glass of water from which he had been sipping. "I want to talk about that study, the one that shows whites and African-Americans still don't have an equal standard of living. I read about that study and it made me angry, it made me sad. We live in a country where we claim to believe in equality, but the economic truths don't support it. Now we can stand here and make speeches about how much we care, but it's all just talk until we're willing to put our money where our mouths are. We need to rebuild our inner cities and we need to recommit to fully funding necessary social programs. And that's why I've devised this five-point plan to reduce the deficit and revitalize our national economy. First of all—"

"Sorry, Senator, you're out of time," said Riviera, smoothing back his moustache with the thumb and middle finger of his left hand. "But the next question is for you. Senator, the crime rate in this country is spiraling out of control. The vice president has recently accused you of being soft on crime. How do you respond?"

The senator took a deep breath. "I'm aware of what the vice president said in his speech the other day. But if the crime situation has gotten out of hand, let's not forget that it happened on the Republican watch, not on ours. They can't blame me. I haven't even taken office yet." There was only a slight murmur of amusement from the audience. "But seriously," the senator continued, "the reason crime has risen in our inner cities is because of the bleak economic forecast and the fact that many of our young people have lost hope in the American dream. Crime, poverty, the economy…they're all interconnected. That's why I've proposed a five-point—"

"Sorry, Senator, you're out of time. Governor?"

"Well, the only thing I have to say is you don't punish criminals by giving them government handouts. You do it by kicking their butts. Any damn fool knows that. I've said it before and I'll say it again. Criminals should be behind bars, where they belong."

The governor paused and suddenly a mischievous glint appeared in his eyes. "And say, Phil, in the few moments I have remaining, how do you think your audience would like a special treat? You know, not many folks know this, but I blow a pretty mean harp." The governor produced a harmonica from the inner breast pocket of his jacket. "What do you say, folks? Anyone want to hear my rendition of 'Achy Breaky Heart?'"

The studio audience roared its approval and the governor launched into the song, his cheeks puffed up like a hamster's and his face red from exertion. When he finished and put down the harmonica, the audience cheered wildly.

"Thank you, Governor," said Riviera, feeling back in his true element for the first time since the broadcast had begun. "Thanks for being such a good sport. That's all the time we have, folks. Thank you Senator Mondukis and Governor Stonewall and thanks to all of you for joining us. And don't miss The Phil Riviera Show tomorrow afternoon when our topic will be transvestite lawyers. See you then!"

Ten seconds after the debate ended, the television commentators were already providing their analyses to the American viewing public and the consensus seemed to be that the governor had "won." According to the commentators, Senator Mondukis looked weak and "needed to work on his timing." He came across as nervous and at one point even appeared to have sweat on his upper lip. Governor Stonewall, on the other hand, displayed far more charisma and everyone seemed to agree that his one-liners were superior. Further, his unexpected bit of whimsy at the end of the debate demonstrated that he wasn't just another politician, that he wasn't afraid to be different, and that he really knew how to work a crowd.

In a room backstage at the television studio, Scoop and Earl stood before a video monitor, flipping back and forth between channels.

"Reg isn't going to like this," said Earl, biting his lip and shaking his head nervously from side to side.

Scoop glanced towards the door. "From the looks of things, I'd say you're right."

Reginald staggered into the room, his face drained of all color and twisted in exasperation. Bret followed directly behind him and was clearly attempting to comfort him. They were dressed in nearly identical dark blue suits and despite the difference in their facial expressions Scoop thought he had never seen them look so much alike.

"It's all right," Bret was saying. "Everything's going to be all right."

"It's *not* all right," Reginald insisted. "Did you hear them? Did you hear what they're saying on television? They're saying he won! They're saying he won the debate!"

"It's okay, Reg," said Scoop. "Calm down."

Reginald shook his head. "I'm sorry, Scoop. I just can't take it anymore."

"Can't take it anymore," said Bret.

Reginald spun around suddenly to face his brother. "And will you stop repeating everything I say! Goddamn it, you're driving me crazy! It's like being followed by a fucking parrot. I'm sick and tired of you hanging on my every word and riding on my goddamn coattails!"

"Coattails?" said Bret. "My dear brother, I'll have you know I pull my weight in this partnership. I *more* than pull my weight. Need I remind you who covered for you when you decided to go through puberty during the McGavin campaign?"

"Puberty?" said the governor, suddenly appearing in the doorway. "Don't tell me you little shits are going through puberty right in the middle of my campaign!"

"No, we are *not* going through puberty, you overstuffed windbag!" said Reginald. "My loving brother here was just rubbing the past in my face, that's all. Evidently forgetting that there are plenty of tales I could tell about *him*!"

"Oh, is that how you want to play it?" asked Bret. "Why you—"

"Boys, boys…," said Scoop.

Reginald was more excited than Scoop had ever seen him, his voice high and shrill like a deranged choirboy's. "I can't take it anymore! I just can't take it! It's all going wrong! Everything's gone wrong!" Suddenly he threw himself to the floor and began kicking his legs and pounding the carpet with his fists. "Wrong, wrong, wrong, wrong, wrong!"

There was a prolonged moment of stunned silence as everyone stared at Reginald, lying face down on the carpet in his hand-tailored suit, his fingers dug deeply into his disheveled hair. And then finally, with as much dignity as he could manage under the circumstances, Reginald pulled himself clumsily back to his feet. He stood brushing the lint from his clothing, his face red, his eyes avoiding everyone.

"Terribly sorry for that…bit of unpleasantness," he said quietly.

"Reg, are you…okay?" asked Scoop.

Reginald displayed a smile that was clearly forced. "Perfectly well, my good man. Perfectly fine. Just lost control for a moment there. Nothing to be concerned about. We can handle this. We can handle this. Perfectly all right. We can handle this."

"Are you sure?" said Scoop. "Maybe you should sit down."

"I'm fine now, I assure you. In fact, I've had a bit of an inspiration. I know precisely what we need to do. It's so simple, so straightforward, so utterly foolproof that it amazes me we didn't think of it before. You see, our problem up until now is that we've been too subtle. Hints of corruption, embarrassing misstatements—the voters can't be bothered with such details. But there's one thing that always gets their attention. Voters have been known to forgive their elected officials for lying, cheating, abusing power in all sorts of ways. But this one thing they never forgive. It's so sensational every newspaper gives it a front-page headline and so uncomplicated that even the most simple-minded can grasp it."

Reginald crossed the room to where the governor was standing and looked directly into his eyes. "Governor," he said, "you're about to be involved in a sex scandal."

11/ California, June 7ᵗʰ

Scoop really didn't mind sitting through Bret's weekly report on campaign finances because the meeting was always conducted first thing in the morning and it allowed him a chance to catch a few extra minutes of sleep. Scoop discovered that if he propped his head up with his hand and wore dark glasses, he could actually snooze a mere three feet away from Bret without anyone in the room being any the wiser. Provided Scoop didn't snore.

"...so concludes my explication of the campaign finance laws regarding the disbursement of federal matching funds," Bret was saying to a chorus of yawns. "Now let us focus our attention, if you would be so kind, on the more immediate implications of said statutes."

Scoop momentarily roused himself from his slumber and leaned towards Earl, seated beside him on the couch in Reginald's hotel suite.

"Is he done yet?" said Scoop in a low voice.

"Not yet," whispered Earl.

"Hmph," said Scoop and tried hard to slip back into unconsciousness.

"By the end of April, we had been able to raise approximately ten million dollars," Bret continued, "thereby making us eligible for an additional 4.78 million in federal matching funds. According to our financial records, we had already expended close to fourteen million on the campaign. In reality, of course, we actually only spent in the neighborhood of eleven million, thereby leaving us with a hardly insignificant profit in excess of three and a half million, approximately two-thirds of which was from direct contributions and the remainder from matching funds." Bret waved a computer-generated pie chart before his audience like a backwoods preacher brandishing a bible.

"Unfortunately," he went on, "as healthy as that profit margin may have appeared, it was lower than originally anticipated. The unexpected longevity of the governor's campaign has regrettably forced us to outlay a larger amount of capital than we had budgeted. This, of course, is what led us to the intensive fund-raising efforts of the past month." Like some sort of nerd magician, Bret produced another pie chart from behind his back, his smile leaving no doubt as to how pleased he was with himself. "And this, gentlemen, is where we stand today. Thanks to a schedule of close to twenty fund-raisers, we have amassed a gross profit of approximately two and a half million dollars for the month of May. Thank you, gentlemen, for your attention."

Earl nudged Scoop with his elbow. "*Now* is he done?" Scoop asked.

"He's done," whispered Earl.

"Fascinating presentation, Bret," said Scoop, removing his sunglasses.

"Thank you, Scoop," said Bret. "I'm overjoyed that you liked it. I was so worried that you and the others might find it a trifle... well, dry."

"Not at all," Scoop assured him. "Spellbinding."

Indeed, it *had* been a prosperous month, with all thoughts of sabotaging the governor's campaign effectively put on hold in order to allow time for raising additional revenues. But now that June had arrived, and with it the rapidly approaching California primary, it was time for the campaign staff to turn its attention back to the impending sex scandal or, as Scoop had been referring to it, Operation Bimbo.

Unfortunately, much to everyone's surprise, the governor seemed suddenly reluctant to cooperate with the scheme. Reginald, perplexed, demanded to know why.

The governor spoke hesitatingly, searching for the right words. "I don't...it's just that...hell, I don't know. I mean, we've come so far. Are you sure this is what we should be doing at this point in the campaign?"

Reginald was more perplexed than ever. "Of course it is. My good man, whatever are you talking about? Don't you want the campaign to be over as soon as possible?"

"Well, sure," said the governor. "Sure I do. Of course."

"Well?" said Reginald. "What then?"

"It's just that…well…" The governor seemed to be searching for words again until, suddenly, his face brightened. "My wife! That's it. It's my wife. When she finds out about this thing, she'll kill me. Quit me for sure, I reckon. That's why I can't go through with it. On account of my wife."

Scoop rolled his eyes. "Now wait a goddamn minute. You've been married for how long? Forty, forty-five years? And you're telling us in all that time you never grabbed a little action on the side?"

The governor furrowed his brow, the picture of righteous indignation. "First of all, you're talking about the woman I married, the mother of my children, and I would never, ever cheat on her. And secondly, if I *had* cheated on her, I'd make damn sure she'd never find out about it. And in this case, she's *guaranteed* to!"

"Oh, yes, I see your ethical dilemma," said Scoop.

"But what if it were explained to her?" suggested Reginald. "That it was only for the good of the campaign, that it didn't actually mean anything?"

The governor snorted. "I'll be damned if I'm going to try feeding her a line like that. She'd think I was just making the whole thing up, using it as an excuse to nail some ass. Sorry, boys. No way. You want to go through with this thing, you all better go talk to her yourselves."

"All right," said Reginald. "All right, we shall. Scoop, I think you should go talk to the governor's wife."

Scoop jerked his head up. "*Me*? Why *me*?"

"Why not?" said Reginald.

So Scoop found himself assigned the unenviable task of explaining to Pat Stonewall, the governor's wife, why it was absolutely necessary for her husband to have sex with another woman and, further, for the affair to be plastered all over the front pages of every newspaper in the country.

Pat hadn't participated in the governor's campaign very much, aside from the occasional appearance at a rally or fund-raiser. But as luck would have it, she was in California to give a speech to the Oakland PTA in support of her husband's candidacy. Scoop took the shuttle from Los Angeles to San Francisco in order to meet with her.

At the appointed time, he appeared at the door of her hotel room in Oakland. She answered the door in a simple green dress, a look of bland good cheer on her face. Scoop couldn't help thinking she resembled an over aged Girl Scout.

"Mr. Heidelman, please come in," she said. "I'll call room service and have some coffee sent up."

"No, no, please don't bother," said Scoop as he stepped tentatively through the doorway. He noticed immediately the general tidiness of the room, how all the bags had been unpacked and stored out of sight, how the bed was neatly made and fresh flowers were arranged in a vase on the table next to the woman's bed. It all seemed so proper and genteel compared to the endless clutter that was always to be found in the rooms of the governor and his staff.

"Sorry the place is such a mess," she blushed, picking up a folded newspaper from the top of a dresser and dropping it into a wastepaper basket. "Please have a seat."

Scoop glanced around the room. The only place to sit appeared to be the bed. He settled himself uncomfortably on the bedspread.

The governor's wife sat on the opposite side of the bed, both of them turning sideways so they could see each other. "My husband said you had something important to talk about," she said. "He was very mysterious. There's nothing wrong, I hope."

"No, nothing wrong," Scoop assured her.

"Well, thank goodness for that. Are you sure you wouldn't care for some coffee, Mr. Heidelman?"

"No, really. Nothing for me." Scoop wanted to get this conversation over with as quickly as possible. He had mentally rehearsed what he was going to say all through the flight to San Francisco, but now that he was here, in the woman's hotel room, he suddenly found himself drawing a blank.

"Uh...Mrs. Stonewall, I need to—"

"Pat."

"I'm sorry?"

"Call me Pat."

"Uh, right. Pat. Pat it is. Uh...Mrs. Stonewall, I need to ask for your cooperation regarding a, uh...highly delicate matter."

Pat smiled at him warmly like a mother who was being asked

to help with her child's homework. "Well, of course, you know I'm always willing to help the campaign any way I can. Please go on."

"Uh, right. Mrs. Stonewall, you know about your husband's arrangement with the Worthington's. About how he's fixing to lose the race?"

Pat blushed and lowered her eyes, as if embarrassed to even have knowledge of such chicanery. "Yes, I'm aware of the arrangement."

"Good. Then you must know that things haven't been going as planned. I mean, your husband's campaign has been going on a lot longer than it was supposed to. So we—the Worthingtons and Earl and I—we're trying to find a way to end it as quickly as possible. 'Cause that was the plan all along. See? You can see that, can't you?"

"Yes, of course," said Pat. "None of this is news to me, Joel. And I'm sure that isn't what you came here to tell me, is it?"

"No. No, of course not." Scoop loosened his collar as beads of sweat began forming on his forehead.

"Are you all right, Joel? You look flushed. Would you like some water?"

"Water? No, no thanks. No water. Never touch the stuff."

"I'm sorry? I don't understand."

He looked into her eyes, as guileless as a child's. How the hell was he going to broach the subject? It was like trying to make a pass at June Cleaver. "Uh, look, Mrs. Stonewall, the thing is…we think we've come up with a way to sabotage your husband's campaign for sure, but…but it's going to require a certain…well, *sacrifice* on your part."

"Sacrifice? What kind of sacrifice?"

Scoop ran his hand across the back of his neck, now drenched with sweat. He swore he had been in saunas that were cooler than this room.

"Uh, Mrs., Stonewall…may I call you Pat?"

"Certainly."

"Pat…uh, Mrs. Stonewall…the thing is…that is, what we've decided to do…"

"Please, Joel, just say whatever's on your—"

"We want your husband to have an affair," Scoop blurted.

Pat's expression changed suddenly and she quickly turned her face away from Scoop's.

"Don't get me wrong, Mrs. Stonewall," Scoop said hurriedly. "It's not like your husband wants to have an affair or anything. He doesn't. Want to have an affair, that is. It's just for the campaign, just for the press he'd get, that's all. So it's not like he'd be having a real affair. I mean, it *will* be a real affair, but he won't enjoy it. Honest. We'll make sure of that. He'll hate it. He'll hate it so much, he'll never even think of doing it again. Not that he thinks of it now, because he doesn't. Think of it, I mean."

Scoop spent a long, uncomfortable moment staring at the back of Pat's head, wondering what he should say, wondering if he had said too much already. He opened his mouth several times to speak, but no words came out.

"So my husband sent you here to ask my permission for him to have an affair," Pat said finally, still not looking at him.

"Well, essentially…yes."

Pat let out a soft, cynical chuckle. "As if he ever needed my permission before."

She turned at last to face him again and Scoop saw that her face was transformed. Gone was the girlishness, the relentless good cheer, and in its place was an expression of world-weariness that took him wholly by surprise. Scoop noticed now what he hadn't seen before— the puffy bags beneath her eyes, the wrinkles of age on her forehead, the way her cheeks sagged with loss and regret. She looked at him with eyes that were red and moist and she spoke in a voice so soft that Scoop had to strain to hear her.

"You don't know what it's like. You have no idea. The fancy dinners, the ceremonies, rubbing elbows with all sorts of important people. Folks think that's what it's all about. They think that's what my life is really like. But they don't know. They don't see."

Pat rose slowly from the bed and walked into the bathroom as if in a trance. When she emerged a moment later, she was carrying a bottle of vodka clutched to her breast, like an actress accepting an award. Imported from Finland, good stuff, Scoop noted. Pat took a glass from the top of the night table and filled it halfway with vodka. She gulped the liquid down quickly, without emotion. Scoop was tempted to ask for some, but thought better of it.

"Have you ever thought what it must be like to be a mannequin, Hr. Heidelman? Always on display, always posing for the cameras, never able to show any real feelings. Because who cares what you're feeling, anyway? As long as your hair is perfect and your make-up is on right... Anyway, that's what it's like being a politician's wife. You hang on his arm and laugh at his jokes and look at him with admiration whenever someone takes a picture of the two of you together. And you keep your mouth shut and your opinions to yourself and you don't make waves. And you make sure never to laugh too loudly at parties or act too aggressive. And for God's sake you never, *ever* do anything that anyone might find inappropriate. But most of all you smile. You smile at your husband and you smile for the cameras and you smile at the crowds when you wave to them. You just keep smiling like an idiot, no matter what you're feeling. That's what it's like, Mr. Heidelman. Like a goddamn mannequin."

She paused for a moment to refill her glass. Her words were coming out in short gasps now and her gaze floated aimlessly around the room. "I think the first time was almost thirty years ago. First time I know of, anyway. The idea of entering politics hadn't even occurred to Thurmond in those days. He was still playing at being the high-powered, big city lawyer. There was a woman in the secretarial pool at his office. A girl, really. Julie, I think her name was. All boobs and no brain, just the way Thurm likes them. Anyway, I think she was the first." Pat brought the glass to her lips and Scoop watched her throat muscles contract and expand as she swallowed equal amounts of vodka and grief.

"Have there been many?" he asked finally.

Pat smiled coldly, cynically. "I've lost count."

"Why...why didn't you leave him?"

She issued a soft chuckle, entirely lacking in mirth. "Where would I go? You think there's anything better out there? No, first I stayed with him because I thought it was just a phase he was going through and he'd outgrow it. Then I stayed with him for the sake of the children. And finally...finally, I stayed with him because I had simply lost the strength to leave." She looked down at the drink in her hand. "That's when this started. I mean, when it *really* started. It's funny, I never used to like drinking alone. Now it turns out that's the only time I drink. *Really* drink. All those parties and receptions when there's champagne being passed around by the gallon and I have to measure it out with an eye dropper. Because I'm playing the role of Mrs. Thurmond Stonewall, the governor's wife, and everyone is watching my every move. It's only when I'm alone that I can really quench my thirst."

"I don't understand," said Scoop. "Didn't you ever at least confront him about his affairs?"

Pat looked at him directly. "Confront him? Thurmond Stonewall? No, I didn't confront him, Mr. Heidelman. I've learned over the years that it isn't a good idea to cross my husband. You have no idea what he's capable of. The cruelty... You don't really know who my husband is. You think you know what you're dealing with, but you don't. You haven't the slightest idea." She said the words as if pronouncing a death sentence.

Scoop found that he could no longer maintain eye contact with the intensity of her glare. Sheepishly, he looked away. "I'm sorry."

"I don't want your pity, Mr. Heidelman. You came here with a question. A request, whatever. Would it be all right with me if my husband had an affair? Yes, Mr. Heidelman, that would be just fine with me. Let him fuck every woman from here to Maine for all I care. There. There's your answer. Satisfied? Now please leave me."

Scoop sat for a moment uncertainly. Surely there was something he should do, something he should say to comfort her, but he had no idea what that might be. Guiltily, without a word, he stood up from the bed and left the room, closing the door behind him.

All the way back to Los Angeles, thoughts of Pat Stonewall crowded Scoop's mind, thoughts that grew angrier and angrier. She had struck a nerve in him, a nerve of pity and compassion, and he resented her for it. What the hell did she have to complain about? She had plenty of options, certainly a hell of a lot more than most people. She was well-off and well-educated, a reasonably attractive Christian white woman in a society that valued such things. She could walk out any time she wanted, file for divorce, start a new life. But no, that would actually require her to *do* something, to take a stand, to step out from the safe, insular world around her and into the fetid air of reality beyond. No, better to play it safe, to stay with her husband, and to continue accepting all the rewards of being a governor's wife—the financial security, the glamour, the fancy wardrobe. Better to complain and do nothing than to actually take action and risk losing what she had. Better to let life pass her by than to actually take a stand.

Scoop gritted his teeth. People create their lives by the choices they make. That's just what they do. Scoop told himself not to feel sorry for Pat Stonewall.

"What the hell are you so moody about?" asked Sarah, startling Scoop from his reverie. It was later that night and they were seated in a Japanese restaurant in downtown Los Angeles. The door of the restaurant was opened wide to the cool of the evening and the breeze rustled the colorful paper screens that had been placed between tables throughout the room to provide a modicum of privacy. Scoop poked at a piece of raw fish with his chopsticks, idly wondering if it was salmon or tuna.

"Do you ever feel as if you're letting your life pass you by?" he asked.

"What?"

"I feel like that sometimes. Like it's easier to stay in a rut than to get out. Like it's easier to be cynical and bitch about something than to actually get off my ass and do something about it."

"My, my, aren't we philosophical tonight?" Sarah snickered and lit a cigarette. "So what are you telling me for? Why don't you go see a psychiatrist or a career counselor or something? Jesus, Scoop, you really can be a downer sometimes, you know that? Besides, politics is your life. If you weren't involved in a campaign, you wouldn't know what to do with yourself."

"Maybe," said Scoop. "Maybe you're right. I guess I just never pictured myself working for someone like the governor."

Sarah's eyes widened at the hint of a story. "What's this? A note of dissent in the Stonewall camp? Do tell."

"Calm down, Sarah. This is strictly off the record. It's just that some of the things the governor says—some of his ad-libs—really make my skin crawl. Race-baiting, gay-bashing, you've heard it all. And I'm his press secretary, for Christ's sake. What does that make me?"

Sarah surveyed him calmly. "I suppose that makes you a racist, sexist, homophobic, Eurocentric scumbag."

Scoop shrugged. "Yeah, well. I don't recycle either. Fuck me."

"Besides," said Sarah, "I think you may be underestimating the governor. I've spent hours interviewing him and he's really a very complicated man."

"Is he now?"

"Yes. As a matter of fact, he's asked me to ghostwrite his autobiography."

"Really. How nice for you. I had no idea the two of you had gotten so chummy."

"Don't be an ass," she said, snuffing out her cigarette in the ashtray. Her watch alarm began beeping and she double-checked the time as she switched it off. "Damn. Quarter to nine already. I've got to get back to my hotel. I'm expecting a call from the East Coast. Thought I might be able to get some paperwork done tonight since it's going to be so dead. And by the way, what the hell is going on tonight? No fund-raisers, no appearances scheduled anywhere. What's the deal?"

Scoop shrugged. "Why don't you ask your good friend, the governor?"

"I did. He was very mysterious. Which only makes me all the more curious."

Scoop sipped from his tiny ceramic cup of sake. "Don't worry, Sarah. I'm sure if anything newsworthy comes out of it, you'll find out about it."

"Oh, great. Thanks for nothing." She snatched up her purse, tossed a twenty onto the table, and turned towards the door. Suddenly, she looked back. "You really don't recycle?"

"I like toxic waste," said Scoop. "I think it should be wrapped in non-recyclable packaging and shipped via non-union delivery services to the homes of well-known lesbians."

"Now you're starting to sound like your boss."

"Yeah," said Scoop. "See you tomorrow."

East of Beverly Hills and west of Hollywood lies a twenty-block stretch of flickering neon known as Sunset Strip, a conglomeration of rock-and-roll nightclubs, topless bars, head shops and fast food restaurants that range from the merely tacky to the outright sordid. It was on this stretch of highway that Scoop and the others hoped to find a willing concubine for the governor—a woman who, unbeknownst to her, was destined to become the leading lady in Operation Bimbo.

The plan was simple enough. In order to avoid drawing attention to himself, the governor agreed to wait back at the hotel while Scoop and the others cruised Sunset Strip looking for prostitutes. When they found one that was suitable, they would offer her a generous fee for a night's work and bring her back to the hotel to meet the governor. Word of the woman's visit would then be leaked to the press, who would be waiting outside the door of the governor's hotel room early the next morning when the lady attempted to make her departure. There would be a flurry of outraged headlines lambasting the governor for his indiscretion (and with his own staff effectively pimping for him—tsk, tsk) and the governor would drop out of the race, leaving the woman to deal with a barrage of book deals and TV-movie offers that would presumably more than compensate her for any embarrassment she might have suffered during the ordeal. Scoop was especially looking forward to seeing the expression on Sarah's face when she found out about the incident. A very complicated man, indeed.

So it was that Scoop found himself driving down Sunset Strip late that night in a rented Ford Escort, he and Earl in the front seat and the Brothers Worthington riding in back. There was only one difficulty with their plan. Even though the governor was waiting back in his hotel room, he insisted upon monitoring their progress via cell phone. And he further insisted upon exercising veto power over any and all of his staff's choices.

"Call girl at ten of clock," said Earl.

Scoop glanced out the windshield towards his right. Up ahead on the sidewalk was a dark-haired Puerto Rican woman wearing a black leather miniskirt, high heels, and a halter top that advertised her cleavage with all the subtlety of a billboard. He pulled the car over to the curb, far enough up the street so she wouldn't immediately approach them.

"Jackpot, Governor," said Scoop into his cell phone. "We've got one in our sights."

"Yeah?" said the governor. "What's she look like? Describe her to me."

"Uh. . .she's in her twenties, I guess. Long hair. Trim. Nice figure."

"She a looker?" asked the governor.

"Of course she's a hooker," said Scoop.

"No, a *looker*."

"Oh." Scoop noticed the outline of the woman's slightly hardened nipples pressing through the thin fabric of her halter top and, when she turned, the way her tight skirt clung to the curve of her rear. He became aware of a faint stirring in his lap. "Well, she works for me."

"How 'bout her knobs?" asked the governor.

"Her what?"

"You know, her knobs, her knockers, her jugs, her hooters. What are her tits like?"

"Oh. Um…big."

"How big is big?" pressed the governor.

"Christ, Governor, you want me to get out of the car and measure them for you?"

"Would you do that?"

"No, I *won't* do that!" snapped Scoop. "Governor, it doesn't make any *difference* what she looks like."

"Maybe not to you, boy," said the governor. "You ain't the one gonna be sticking your pole in her. Besides, tomorrow morning her picture's gonna be on every front page in the country and everyone's gonna know I diddled the bitch. And I'll be damned if she's gonna be some kind of dog!"

"Okay, okay, Governor," said Scoop, "Calm down. She's not a dog."

"She a blond?"

"What? No, she's not a—she's a brunette."

"Well, forget it then," said the governor. "Go find me a blond."

"Oh, for Christ's sake, Governor," Scoop protested, "what's the diff—"

"It's a blond or nothing," the governor insisted.

"All right, all right," said Scoop, "Jesus fucking Christ."

"And stop taking the name of the lord in vain, boy," said the governor.

"Oh, sorry, Governor," said Scoop sarcastically. "Didn't realize you were so religious."

Scoop swung the car around and headed in the opposite direction on Sunset Strip. He drove about three blocks down until he spotted a young blond woman, standing in the glow of a neon sign that read GOOD EATS.

Got that right, thought Scoop. She was about twenty-five, he guessed, dressed in a black leather corset with stiletto heels and fishnet stockings with garters. Her hair was blown back away from her face and she must have been wearing the reddest lipstick Revlon manufactured. Demurely situated on her left cheek was a beauty mark which, Scoop guessed, was probably more the product of cosmetics than genetics. The Madonna look. Scoop pulled over.

"Okay, Governor," said Scoop, "we've got her. Ms. Right."

"And just how can you tell that?" asked the governor.

"Trust me," said Scoop. "She's just what you're looking for. Madonna."

"That her name?"

"No, that's what she looks like."

"Oh." There was a pause. "You mean the singer, right? Not the other one."

"Right," said Scoop. "The singer."

"Hmm," said the governor. "That don't sound half bad. Okay, I'll bite. Bring her in."

"Thank God," said Scoop, snapping shut the phone. "Earl, roll down the window and tell her we want to do some business."

Earl jumped as if someone had dropped a lit cigarette down the front of his pants. "What? I...I can't do that! I'm a married man."

"Earl, it's not for you, it's for the governor," Scoop reminded him. "We're just negotiating the deal."

"That's besides the point," Earl pleaded. "I've...I've never done this before. I wouldn't know what to say."

"Oh, for... Look, just roll down the window and call her over, okay? I'll handle everything else."

Earl rolled down the window. "Uh...excuse me! Miss? Can we have a word with you?"

She approached the car shakily, so unsteady on her stiletto heels she twice nearly toppled from the curb. It was only then that Scoop realized she was puckered to the gills.

"What can I do for you boys?" Madonna purred throatily, her words slurred by alcohol. She peered through the passenger side window.

"An even grand for the night," said Scoop. "Just get in. No questions."

She glanced in the backseat and found the faces of Reginald

and Bret smiling nervously back at her. "Wow, talk about kinky," she hiccupped. "I've never done it with twin midgets before."

"No, it's not them," said Scoop. "It's our friend back at the hotel. You game?"

The woman paused for a moment, a mischievous smile playing across her face. "For a thousand bucks? Sure, why not?" She squeezed into the backseat and inserted herself between the Worthingtons, who squirmed to opposite ends of the car seat as if someone had just deposited a wild animal into their midst.

"Boys, boys, calm down," slurred Madonna, the smell of alcohol heavy on her breath. She leaned back and put her right hand on Reginald's left knee and her left hand on Bret's right knee. "I'm not making you boys nervous, am I?"

"No, no, not a bit," Reginald fairly stammered.

"Not a bit, not at all," echoed Bret.

Scoop pulled the car out and headed for the hotel. A few drops of rain hit the windshield in fat, heavy splotches. Scoop clicked on the wipers.

"Gee, starting to rain," Earl observed, just to break the uncomfortable silence that had fallen over the car. "Lucky for you we picked you up when we did."

"Hmph," said Madonna. "Lucky for you I even agreed to do business with someone driving a lousy Escort."

At the hotel, they drove into the underground parking garage and took the rear elevator to the eighth floor. Scoop led the woman to the governor's hotel room and knocked on the door. The governor answered, flashing a smile that was equal parts conspiracy and lust.

"Well hey there, little lady, ain't you a purdy sight. And what might your name be?"

Madonna shrugged. "What do you want it to be?"

"Heh heh. Well I reckon that's as good an answer as any. And I reckon you know who I am."

She looked at him with disinterest. "Why, should I? Hey, you got anything to drink?" She pushed past him and into the room, tossing her purse onto the bed.

The governor turned to Scoop, a scowl on his face. "What the hell does she mean, she doesn't know who I am?" he growled quietly. "What has she been doing, living in a cave somewhere?"

"Calm down, Governor," said Scoop. "Maybe she just doesn't follow the news."

"Doesn't know who I am…," the governor muttered.

"Hey, Jack Daniels!" the woman squealed from within. "I *love* Jack Daniels!" She had discovered the open bottle where the governor had left it, on the edge of the dresser across from the bed. She poured herself a quarter glass and downed it in one gulp.

"I trust you can take it from here?" Scoop asked the governor.

The governor winked at him. "You can count on it, boy."

But half an hour later, as the campaign staff sat drafting the governor's farewell address, the governor suddenly burst into the room, his thin grey hair standing out crazily in all directions and his eyes wild with excitement.

"Goddamn fucking son-of-a-bitch bastard motherfucker shit— it's a man!" he blurted.

For a moment, everyone else just looked at him. "What?" Scoop asked finally. "Governor, what the hell are you talking about?"

"That…that *thing* in my room. It's not a woman!"

"Governor, I'm afraid you aren't being terribly coherent," said Reginald. "Now please compose yourself and tell us what happened."

The governor took a deep breath and made a vain attempt to smooth back his hair, but succeeded only in rearranging it into a different random pattern. "I didn't lay a hand on her. I swear. We were just sitting there drinking. She was really putting it away, too, gulping it down like a fish. Then all of a sudden, she up and passes out. Right there on the bed. So I figure what the hell and I start taking her clothes off. Well, I pull her panties down and what do I see but some guy's pecker staring back at me. For Christ's sake, she's a he!"

Reginald's eyes grew wide with glee. "Why, that's marvelous! This is even better than we'd planned! Imagine the headlines! 'Stonewall Caught in Tryst With Local Drag Queen.' It's almost too perfect to be true!"

Scoop was amazed that someone of the governor's girth could move so quickly. In one fluid motion, Stonewall had shot across the room and grabbed Reginald by the throat. The governor lifted him off the ground so that Reginald's legs dangled spastically in the air.

"Ack," said Reginald. "Gov…you…chok…"

"Damn right I'm choking you, you little shit," said the governor. "I'll be damned if I'm going to have the whole country thinking I'm some kind of fucking faggot. Now you get that goddamn…*freak* out of my hotel room. *Now!*"

"But Governor," pleaded Bret, "it's too late. We've already leaked the word to the press. At any moment, this entire hotel is going to be crawling with reporters."

"What?" The governor let go of Reginald, who stumbled to the ground, and swung around to glare at Bret. "Well, I guess you'd just better get your asses in gear then, boy. 'Cause if you don't, there's going to be another headline in tomorrow's papers. 'Stonewall Murders Entire Campaign Staff.'"

Reginald stood shakily, rubbing his throat, his eyes moist. "All right, Governor. Just calm down. We can handle this. Earl, go bring the car around to the rear elevator. Bret, go find a laundry cart, the kind the chambermaids use. Scoop, you come with me. Everyone move! Fast!"

They burst out of the room and shot off in opposite directions. Scoop and Reginald ran down the hall to the governor's room. Madonna was still passed out on the governor's bed, half-undressed, her panties down around her knees. They hurriedly went about putting her clothes back on. A moment later there was a knock at the door and Bret appeared with a laundry cart.

"Anyone see you?" asked Reginald.

"I don't think so."

Scoop half-carried, half-dragged the body across the room and deposited it in the cart. The heavy cotton sides of the laundry bag bulged. They covered the body with dirty sheets and towels.

Reginald stuck his head out the door and looked both ways. "All clear," he said.

The three of them rolled the cart out of the hotel room and then left, down the corridor, heading for the rear elevator. It began to look as if they just might get away with it.

But halfway down the hall a door opened and out stepped a tall, clean-cut young man in a white shirt and dark blue suit. A Secret Service agent. Fred.

"Good morning," said Fred.

"Morning?" said Reginald, startled. "Oh, why, yes, I suppose it is."

"You're up early," said Fred.

"Yes," said Reginald. "Early. We needed to rise especially early today in order to...uh..." Reginald glanced at the laundry cart beside him. "...do the laundry," he blurted.

The Secret Service agent looked at them for a moment, two sixteen-year-old twins and a middle-aged man, their clothes rumpled and their eyes red from lack of sleep, an identical look of nervous exhaustion on each of their faces.

"Is there anything wrong?" asked Fred.

"Wrong?" said Reginald. "No, of course not, my good man. Why would there be anything wrong?"

"Well, maybe I can call one of the maids to take care of that laundry for you," said Fred.

"No!" Scoop and the Worthingtons all blurted out at once. Fred looked at them curiously.

"Really, it's all right," said Reginald. "No need to disturb the chambermaids at this unholy hour. As long as we're awake, we might as well tend to it ourselves. Besides, it might do us some good. See how the other half lives and all that sort of rubbish."

"Right," said Fred. "Well, be careful."

"Oh, we shall, my good man," said Reginald, "We shall." They proceeded on down the corridor and rounded the corner.

"My lord, that was close," Reginald whispered when they were out of earshot. "Do you think he was suspicious?"

"If he wasn't, then he must have cheated on his Civil Service exam," said Scoop. "But fortunately he's on our side."

They rode the rear elevator down to the underground garage. Earl was waiting for them in the car.

"Hurry up," he said, his voice high-pitched and nervous. "I think I saw Wolf Blitzer in the lobby."

"Get the trunk open," Reginald instructed.

Earl got out and popped the trunk while Scoop pulled Madonna out of the laundry cart and threw him over his shoulder. Hunched over from the weight, he staggered around to the rear of the car and heaved the body into the trunk. One arm and a leg hung clumsily out over the side.

"Well, push it in," said Reginald. "Get the arm and leg in."

"The trunk isn't big enough," said Scoop, wiping sweat from his forehead.

"No, it'll fit," said Reginald, "If you just bend the leg back and push—"

"*It won't fit*," Scoop insisted.

"Oh, bloody hell. Damn it to bloody hell," said Reginald. "Who the hell rented this car?"

"I did," said Earl.

"Well how could you be so bloody stupid?"

"How was I supposed to know?" Earl shouted. "What was I supposed to say? Make sure you give me a car with a trunk large enough to fit a body? It's a goddamn Escort, for Christ's sake."

"Enough," said Scoop. "We haven't got time for this now. Help me get her into the backseat."

"Shouldn't that be *him*?" corrected Bret.

"Bret, shut the hell up and grab a leg," said Scoop.

Together they pulled the body out of the trunk and threw it into the backseat, the Worthingtons climbing in after it and Scoop and Earl taking the front. Scoop turned the ignition key and gunned the engine just as a camera crew in an NBC van came barreling into the garage.

"Go!" said Reginald.

Scoop hit the gas and the car spun out across the parking garage, passing the NBC van traveling in the opposite direction. He hit the exit ramp to the street above at about fifty miles an hour and the sudden incline made the bottom of the car slam against the concrete, sending a shower of sparks in all directions. At the top of the ramp, someone had placed a wooden roadblock.

"Don't stop," commanded Reginald.

They hit the roadblock at full speed, sending wooden splinters through the air and tearing off part of the front bumper. The tires squealed as Scoop threw the car into a hard right and headed off in the direction of Sunset Boulevard.

The rain had stopped and the first light of dawn was just beginning to peek over the horizon as they sped east on Sunset Strip towards Hollywood. They had done it, snuck a drunken transvestite out of the governor's hotel room right under the noses of hotel security, the

Secret Service, and all three major news networks. The only problem now was what to do with the body.

"I must say I fail to see what difference it makes," said Reginald from the backseat. "Leave it anywhere. A park bench, a bus stop. Who cares?"

"She's passed out drunk, Reg," Scoop reminded him. "Can you really guarantee she's going to be safe on a park bench in this city?"

"Why do you persist in referring to it as *her*," asked Bret, "when its masculine identity has, at this point, been clearly established?"

"I think you're being totally unreasonable, Scoop," said Reginald, ignoring his brother. "For God's sake, it isn't *our* responsibility. Why can't we just leave it in a dumpster somewhere?"

"I am not going to leave a human being in a dumpster," Scoop snapped.

"Fine," said Reginald. "Have it your way. Drive around all morning if you like. But mind you, the later it gets the more difficult it becomes to dispose of it without being seen."

They entered the Hollywood Hills and on a whim Scoop took a left, heading east on Highland Avenue. Signs for the Hollywood Bowl began appearing along the roadside. Suddenly Scoop spotted a marquee with the words: APPEARING LIVE THIS WEEKEND ONLY—MADONNA—THE DO IT TILL YOU GO BLOND TOUR.

"Got it," said Scoop. He veered left through one of the large parking lots adjacent to the Bowl and then through the entrance, swinging around to the back of the shell that rose huge and majestic behind the stage. Almost immediately, a security guard was upon them, a lanky kid with bleary eyes and a face full of peach fuzz.

"Can't park here, man," the kid called to them as he approached. He was dressed in faded denim jeans and a navy blue Hollywood Bowl shirt to indicate he was a member of the staff.

"Nobody else say a word," Scoop cautioned the others as he killed the engine. "Hey, kid," he called to the guard, "we've got an emergency over here."

"You gotta get out of here," said the guard, lowering his voice as he reached the car. "General public ain't allowed back here."

Scoop got out of the driver's seat and stood facing him. "General public? Christ, can't you see who we've got in the backseat?"

The guard squinted uncertainly, then leaned down and glanced through the window.

"Holy shit!" he said. "What the hell happened to her?"

"Never mind that," said Scoop. "Just get her inside and let her sleep it off."

"Sure," stammered the guard. "Sure thing."

Scoop opened the back door and the Worthingtons passed the body out. Despite his apparent scrawniness, the guard easily lifted her in his arms.

"I suggest," said Scoop, getting back in the driver's seat, "that you treat her very, *very* nicely. She's had a rough night."

"Right," said the guard. "I mean, of course. But who...who are you, man?"

Scoop slammed the door and started the engine. "Just a music lover," he said. He threw the car into drive and burned rubber all the way back to Sunset Boulevard.

Coming back into downtown Los Angeles, Scoop's cell phone rang. It was the governor.

"You boys got everything taken care of?"

"Yes, Governor," said Scoop, not even trying to hide the exhaustion in his voice. "Everything's taken care of. We're coming in. How's everything back at the hotel?"

"All clear," said the governor. "Bunch of reporters hanging around like vultures outside my hotel room, but they all took a powder soon as they found out there wasn't any blood." The governor chuckled. "Now how do you figure something like that? Pick yourself up a pretty little gal and she turns out to be some kind of weirdo in drag."

"Yeah, well, I guess it just goes to show you can't believe everything you see," said Scoop.

"You got that straight, boy," said the governor. "Goddamn son of a bitch wasn't even a natural blond."

12/ Texas, June 21st

"Did you hear about that Madonna thing?" Sarah had asked. "Weird, huh?"

She had pointed to the headline of The Daily American that read: MADONNA REALLY A MAN. ("I wonder if Sean knew," Scoop had thought fast enough to quip.) The story went on to reveal that, despite the misleading headline, it was not the real Madonna being referred to, but an impersonator. According to the story, a man had disguised himself as Madonna in order to gain access to her dressing room when she had appeared recently at the Hollywood Bowl. He actually succeeded in passing himself off as the famous performer and even managed to spend some time sleeping in her dressing room, but was discovered as an imposter later the next day when a guard found him standing before a urinal in the men's room. When questioned by the police, the man insisted that he didn't know how he had ended up in Madonna's dressing room and clung to a bizarre story about having been kidnapped by twin dwarves the night before. The man was being held by the Los Angeles Police Department pending the results of a psychiatric evaluation. In the meantime, his lawyer dealt with a barrage of book deals and TV-movie offers.

But it was another publication, just to the left on the newsstand, that had demanded Scoop's attention. For Time Magazine featured the governor himself on its cover and emblazoned above the color photograph ran a headline in yellow capital letters that read WHAT DOES THURMOND WANT? Inside, the magazine contained a feature story in which the writer speculated as to precisely why the governor was still in the race for the Democratic nomination. While the governor clearly didn't have enough delegates to take the convention, the article pointed out, he did have enough clout and press attention to be a spoiler. Did the governor simply want to play the role of power broker? Or was he planning to lead a revolt at the convention? The writer suggested various scenarios and one of the magazine's political analysts discussed the possibility of a brokered convention in detail. But ultimately, no one could say for sure why the governor was still in the race.

Including, for that matter, the governor's own staff. With the Democratic National Convention just a month away, Reginald anxiously awaited word from Felix Greene that it was time for the governor to call it quits. But the call from Greene hadn't come yet and Greene, no doubt preoccupied with the minutiae of the upcoming convention, wasn't even responding to Reginald's numerous telephone calls.

Now that the primary season was over, the whole gang was back in Texas, holed up in a hotel in Austin. As usual, they had rented a number of rooms, all on the same floor. Even the governor was keeping a room there, despite the fact that his ranch was just on the outskirts of the city, less than an hour's drive away. He claimed that he wanted to be close to his campaign staff, so that they could meet at short notice if they needed to. But the explanation didn't ring true to Scoop because, in fact, the governor rarely bothered to attend staff meetings anymore, preferring instead to stay in his room and "prepare his memoirs," which Scoop took to be a euphemism for drinking bourbon and napping. Scoop wondered if the real reason the governor was staying at the hotel didn't have more to do with a possible rift between the Stonewalls in the wake of Operation Bimbo, but Scoop had no real evidence to support his suspicion.

Indeed, sometimes Scoop wouldn't even see the governor for days at a time. And then, one evening as Scoop entered the hotel restaurant in hopes of grabbing a quick dinner, he encountered the governor standing just inside the doorway, surrounded by an entourage of Secret Service agents. The governor seemed to be in a particularly jovial state of mind. He flashed a toothy grin and motioned for Scoop to come closer.

"I've been chowing down in my room, for the most part," the governor explained, "but I was starting to feel like a horned owl locked up in a chicken coop. So I thought I'd come down here.

They're just getting a room in the back ready for me. Say, I was planning on eating alone. Why don't you join me?"

Scoop thought for a moment. The idea of having dinner alone with the governor didn't exactly thrill him, but he also wasn't in the mood to start searching for another place to eat.

"Sure," said Scoop. "Why not?"

They were seated in a private room at the back of the restaurant, the Secret Service agents standing guard outside the door. A white-jacketed waiter arrived to take their order, a young Mexican man with a thin moustache and an olive complexion.

"How are the ribs tonight, José?" the governor asked him while surveying the menu.

"Please, sir," the waiter responded, "my name is Mañuel."

"Aw c'mon, boy, I'm just riding you a little," the governor chuckled. "How are the ribs? Nice and juicy, just the way I like 'em?"

"Yes, sir," said Mañuel. "Ribs are our specialty."

"Good," said the governor. "How about these here mashed potatoes? They made from scratch? They ain't made from that powdered crap, are they? I can't stand that powdered crap."

"No, sir," said Mañuel. "Everything we serve is homemade."

"Good. Let me have an order of ribs and beans with a side of mashed potatoes. And corned bread. Plenty of corned bread," said the governor.

"Very good, sir," said Mañuel. "And you?"

Scoop shrugged. "What the hell. I'll have the same. And a Dewey on the rocks."

"How are the memoirs coming?" Scoop asked the governor after the waiter had disappeared.

"The what? Oh, yeah, the memoirs. Going good, going damn good, matter of fact. I may even wind up with a bestseller on my hands. 'Course, that's once I get everything…you know…whipped into shape."

"Right," said Scoop. "Whipped into shape."

The waiter brought their food, plates piled high with steaming meat and beans. He turned to go as Scoop sampled one of the ribs, sticky sweet with a mixture of barbeque sauce and grease, while the governor took a huge forkful of mashed potatoes.

An instant later, the governor spat the potatoes out. "Hey, José!" he called. "Get your ass back in here!"

Manuel's face again appeared in the doorway. "Did you call me?" he blinked, as if not quite sure what he had heard. "Is anything wrong?"

"You're damn right something's wrong," the governor chuckled derisively. "These goddamn mashed potatoes are what's wrong."

"I'm sorry?" said Manuel.

"You told me these potatoes were made from scratch, José," said the governor. "Not from that powdered crap. I hate that powdered crap. Told you that right up front. Didn't I tell you that right up front, boy?"

"Governor, please," said Scoop, embarrassed by his companion's behavior. "It isn't that big a deal."

"It's a big deal if I say it is," the governor replied calmly. "I can't stand that powdered crap."

"Sir, these are the same mashed potatoes we serve everyone," Manuel nervously assured him. "If you'd like to talk to our chef…"

"No, I don't want to talk to the goddamn chef, José," said the governor, his voice beginning to rise. "I'm talking to you. You're the one who told me these here mashed potatoes were made from scratch. Which, if you actually tasted them, you'd know they ain't." The governor threw his fork down in disgust.

"Governor, please," said Scoop. "That's enough. Let it go."

"I won't let it go," said the governor. "I was promised homemade mashed potatoes and that's what I'll have, goddamn it."

"Sir, I've already told you, these are the only mashed potatoes we have," said Manuel, a hint of anger beginning to creep into his voice.

"Oh, is that so?" said the governor, "Is that so? Well you can feed it to the goddamn dogs, 'cause I sure as hell ain't eating it." With a flick of his wrist, the governor grabbed his plate by the rim and tossed it off the table. It bounced slightly as it hit the carpeted floor, the food splattering in all directions and forming a colorful abstract pattern on the carpet. Both Scoop and the waiter froze, stunned by the governor's action.

Mañuel regained his senses a moment later. "I...I'd better get something to clean that up."

"I'd say you better," the governor echoed. "And get me another dinner. With real mashed potatoes this time."

"Sir, I already told you—" Mañuel stopped and heaved a sigh of exasperation. "Yes, sir. Anything you say."

"Don't you get smart with me, boy," scolded the governor. "You show some respect for your elders. I ain't some kind of goddamn clown."

Mañuel turned towards the door. His voice came softly, under his breath, almost too quiet to be heard. "Could have fooled me."

"Hey, I heard that, you little spic bastard!" snapped the governor.

Mañuel froze, one step away from the door.

"Governor, please..." said Scoop.

But it was too late. The governor had leapt up from the table and grabbed the waiter by the scruff of his neck. He twisted Mañuel's right arm back and up until the wrist was practically touching the back of the man's neck. Mañuel grimaced in pain as the governor forced him to his knees.

"You like those mashed potatoes so much, José?" said the governor. "Huh? Do you? Then why don't you eat them? Huh, boy? Just go ahead and eat them." Holding the man's wrist fast in the grip of his left hand, he used his right hand to push Mañuel's face down towards the pile of mashed potatoes smeared across the carpet.

"Governor!" Scoop sprang up from the table and grabbed the governor from behind, trying to pull him off of the other man, as a cadre of Secret Service agents burst through the door at the sound of the commotion.

"Go ahead, you little shit!" the governor shouted. "Eat it! Eat it!"

Scoop replayed the scene in his mind many times over the next few days. It seemed surreal, like an outtake from a David Lynch movie or a Donald Rumsfeld press conference. Scoop had known that the governor possessed a quick temper, but he had never before seen anyone erupt over something so seemingly insignificant. To Scoop, the incident once again brought to mind questions regarding the governor's mental stability.

"Reginald, have you ever thought that the governor might be a little…well, unbalanced?"

They were sitting in Reginald's hotel room, he and Reginald and Bret and Earl. Reginald had decided to shave that morning, something he did infrequently due to the lightness of his beard. Unfortunately, his inexperience in performing the task had led him to cut himself in several places and now his face was dotted with blots of white toilet paper. In addition, ever since the close call at the hotel in Los Angeles, Reginald was becoming increasingly paranoid about the possibility that members of the press might uncover their scheme and had therefore gotten into the practice of routinely searching his room for hidden microphones. It was precisely this ritual which Reginald was performing when Scoop asked his question. Reginald stopped and looked at him.

"Unbalanced? How do you mean?"

"You know, *unbalanced*," said Scoop. "As in crazy."

Reginald snickered. "My good man, don't be absurd. The governor is no more unbalanced than you or I," his voice echoing from the bathroom as he carefully studied the inside of the toilet. The thought gave Scoop very little comfort.

They had assembled that morning to discuss Reginald's latest idea: the selection of the governor's running mate. Reasoning that the governor himself appeared to be insulated from any trace of scandal by a seemingly impenetrable layer of Teflon, Reginald decided that it might be a good idea for the governor to associate himself with someone who was considerably more vulnerable to the vagaries of public opinion. Reginald noted that the selection of Thomas Eagleton in 1972 had helped to torpedo the candidacy of George McGovern (and Scoop cringed to even hear the name mentioned in such a context) and that, twenty years later, neither George Bush, Sr. nor Ross Perot had exactly benefited from being associated in the minds of voters with their respective running mates. Besides, Reginald pointed out, coming from a candidate who wasn't even favored to win his party's nomination, the announcement of a running mate would be seen by some political observers as the height of arrogance.

So the governor's campaign staff set about the task of choosing the worst possible vice presidential candidate. As tempting as they were, Dan Quayle and Admiral Stockdale were immediately ruled out as being too obvious, while Ed Meese and John Sununu didn't make the cut because of their party affiliation.

"How about Buckton, that Congressman from West Virginia who got convicted for influence peddling last week?" said Earl.

"An inspired suggestion, Earl," said Reginald, "but I prefer Senator Pinholster from Wyoming. As you may recall, he was recently indicted for both influence peddling and having sex with a minor."

"Sure, but he was only *indicted,*" argued Earl. "Buckton has already been *convicted.*"

"True enough," Reginald countered, "but if Pinholster is convicted, his accumulated jail time would surely exceed Buckton's."

Scoop found it difficult to stay focused on the conversation; his mind was caught in a whirlwind of unrelated fears and desires. Was the governor really nuts? Despite Reginald's assurances to the contrary, Scoop still had his doubts. He replayed the scene that had transpired between the governor and the waiter once again, then drifted back to the bus ride to Philadelphia during which he had sat next to the governor. It wasn't even the idea that the governor might be a bit loony that bothered him so, Scoop realized. After all, lots of people were a little eccentric. Scoop had had a great uncle who, in his later years, began having prolonged conversations with his pet parakeet, sometimes when the bird wasn't even present. The old man clearly didn't pose a threat to anyone, including himself, and hence the rest of the family chose to ignore the odd behavior. But the governor's particular brand of dementia, if in fact that's what it was, didn't seem nearly so benign. Rather, there was a heavy air of malevolence to it, a real threat of violence that seemed to pulsate from within. Once again Scoop thought of the mysterious brown satchel the governor had been carrying that morning in Philadelphia. Scoop hadn't seen the bag in some time; he wondered whether the governor still had it.

Scoop's mind turned to the outcome of the campaign. Despite his low number of delegates, the governor still seemed to be doing relatively well in the polls, having won the support of many independent and disaffected voters as well as conservative Democrats who found Mondukis too liberal for their tastes. This despite his staff's numerous attempts to sabotage the governor's campaign and the fact that the governor had yet to clearly spell out his position on any subject of real importance. Scoop was once again gripped by an eerie sense of inevitability, of being caught in the flow of a predetermined history that he didn't fully understand, a history so vast and all-encompassing that Scoop couldn't even clearly see his own role in it, couldn't see the way all the people and elements within it connected because he was still entangled in it himself.

And that alone gave him pause, the idea that he might someday be remembered as the press secretary of the Stonewall campaign and that, for some vague reason still beyond his grasp, history might one day assign some importance to the fact that he had played that role. To have his name linked with Stonewall's for the rest of history—the very thought made Scoop nauseous. And what the hell was he doing in this campaign anyway? This wasn't the reason he had gotten involved in politics. Not to work for the likes of Thurmond Stonewall, certainly not to help inflate the bank accounts of opportunistic scum like the Worthingtons. Where the hell had his idealism gone, his passion, his willingness to risk everything for a cause in which he believed?

When Reginald had mentioned George McGovern just a few minutes before, Scoop had had a sickening feeling deep in the pit of his stomach, a feeling of loss and grief, like when you hear the name of a long-lost lover and can't stop yourself from flinching. Lisa…Lisa Pearlstein. Yes, that was the name of the woman he had known back in college, the name he couldn't remember. It had just now come to him, just like that. Lisa Pearlstein. He wondered where Lisa was now, what she was doing, whether she had a husband and family, and whether or not, during fleeting moments of nostalgia, she ever thought of him just as he did of her.

Scoop saw Reginald's lips moving and certainly heard his voice as it droned on, but made no attempt to attach any meaning to the words, so immersed was he in his own thoughts. His mind turned to Sarah, to the relationship between them. Or was he being too presumptuous in even thinking of it as a "relationship?" For they had never discussed their feelings for each other, had never let their masks of cynicism slip, even when they were alone together. They communicated with each other mostly through wisecracks and a sort of good-natured sarcasm, a language all their own. For one of them to forthrightly reveal any affection for the other would be unthinkable, like reading love poetry to the war buddy with whom you had fought in the trenches. Scoop realized that he honestly had no idea how Sarah felt about him or whether she felt anything at all. He had always planned to reveal his love for her when the campaign was over, after the scam with the Worthingtons was concluded, so as not to put himself in the emotionally untenable position of being honest with her with regard to his feelings while lying to her about the true nature of the governor's campaign. But now he felt himself more and more anxious to know where he really stood with her, to determine whether or not the love he felt growing inside him was, in fact, requited.

"...Pat Stonewall?" Reginald asked him directly.

Scoop blinked. "What? You talking about the governor's *wife* being his running mate? Well, I think it's an interesting idea, but I'm afraid some of the voters might actually approve. You know, they'd think it was charming or romantic or some such bullsh—"

"Scoop, where on earth have you been?" asked Reginald. "We're not discussing running mates anymore. The topic has changed several times already. Really, Scoop, you must make more of an effort to pay attention." He absently picked pieces of toilet paper from his face.

"Sorry," said Scoop. "I was drifting. What are we talking about?"

"We're talking about the governor's wife," said Earl, trying to be helpful.

"I got that much," said Scoop. "What about her?"

"I was suggesting," said Reginald, folding his hands in his lap, "that if we could just get some dirt on Pat Stonewall, it might reflect badly on her husband."

"Dirt?" said Scoop. "What do you mean dirt? What kind of dirt?"

"You know, Scoop," said Bret. "Maybe something in a Betty Ford-Kitty Dukakis sort of vein."

"Yes, precisely," said Reginald. "That's what I was just asking you. You've spoken to the woman recently. What was your impression of her? Are there any proverbial skeletons in the lady's closet? Anything we could use against her?"

Scoop shifted uncomfortably in his seat. "No, nothing I know of."

"Are you sure, Scoop?" pressed Bret, leaning forward on the arm of the chair in which his brother was seated, like a parrot perched on his shoulder. "No nasty habits at all? She doesn't pop pills or anything like that?"

Scoop avoided his glance. "No, I just told you. Nothing like that."

"Think hard, Scoop," said Reginald. "This is important. Are you sure there isn't *anything* at all? Anything that—"

"Goddamn it, I said *no*! How many fucking times do I have to say it? Now back the fuck off!"

Three pairs of eyes stared at him, stunned by his outburst.

"It's all right, Scoop," said Reginald quietly, a look of worried concern on his face. "If you say there's nothing there, there's nothing there. We believe you."

"Oh, fuck you, Reginald. Fuck all of you." Scoop suddenly found himself on his feet and headed towards the door. Reginald jumped from his seat and blocked the way.

"Scoop, old man, what is it?" he said. "Where are you going? What on earth is wrong?"

"I've had it Reg. It's over. Enough."

"What's over? What are you talking about?" asked Reginald.

"Reg, just get the fuck out of my way. Now."

They stood for a moment, silently, just looking at each other, two friends who could both sense that somehow, after this moment, things would never be the same between them. Finally, without a word, Reginald stepped aside. Scoop walked quickly past him and out the door.

Standing alone in the hallway, Scoop pondered his next move. He hadn't intended for it to happen this way, but this was how it had happened. So be it. Scoop had no idea what the future held for him. Maybe he would get out of politics entirely, he didn't know. All he knew is that he would never again work for a candidate like Thurmond Stonewall. That part of his life was over. For the first time in decades, Scoop felt truly free. There was no turning back now. From here on out, it was every man for himself.

First, Scoop decided, he would type his letter of resignation. Nothing terribly complicated, maybe just *To Whom It May Concern, I Quit* and his signature. He would deliver it to Reginald within the hour. Then he would call Sarah's room and insist on seeing her immediately. He would reveal his feelings to her openly, without shame or hesitation, and demand to know whether or not she felt the same. And then, with her or without her, he would board the next flight north and would vow to never again set foot in the godforsaken state of Texas for as long as he lived.

But no. There was something he wanted to do first, something that took priority over all else. He was going to go to the governor's room and tell that self-satisfied bastard exactly what he thought of him. His mind gleefully brimming with every invective he had resisted hurling at the governor for the past year, Scoop headed down the hallway towards the governor's room.

When he got there, he was surprised to find there were no Secret Service agents standing guard outside the door. Why had the governor sent them away? he idly wondered. He pounded on the governor's door, the sound reverberating down the empty hallway. Waited a few moments. Pounded again. Nothing. No sound, no response, nothing. *Fuck.*

Scoop heaved a sigh and turned to go. But suddenly he heard something, a rustling sound, from within the room.

"Governor, are you in there?" Scoop reached for the doorknob. It turned. He swung open the door and stepped inside.

Scoop heard a brief shriek, but everything was moving too fast for him to clearly determine what was happening. All he saw was a wild blur of buttocks and bed sheets and naked breasts. And when the scene before him finally settled, he found himself face-to-face with Sarah, who stood nervously clutching a sheet up to her chin.

"Scoop, will you get the hell out of here?" she demanded.

The governor stood on the other side of the bed. He was dressed in a white, ribbed undershirt and light blue boxer shorts, but he was also wearing a ten-gallon hat and a pair of brown leather cowboy boots.

"What the hell you gawking at, boy?" asked the governor. "Ain't you ever seen a man in his underwear before?"

Scoop felt paralyzed, the room spinning around him, as if he had just had the last drink of the evening and knew he was in for one hell of a hangover the next morning. "I...I'm sorry," he stammered. "I didn't know. I just...I didn't know."

"Scoop, will you please just leave?" said Sarah.

"Yes. Yes...I'm sorry." Scoop stumbled out of the room, closing the door behind him. He stood alone in the hallway, stunned, and the only sound was the click of the governor's door being locked from within.

13/ Texas, July 3rd—Washington DC, July 4th

Scoop hadn't seen the near side of sober in almost two weeks. Everything was a blur, reality slipping in and out of focus haphazardly. Days and nights blended together in an endless cycle of drinking, losing consciousness, waking up, and drinking again, until Scoop could no longer tell the date on the calendar or the day of the week. His mouth was perpetually dry, his head pounded. He couldn't remember when he had last eaten or showered or shaved. Surely he must have performed these mundane tasks at various times if for no other reason than the sheer force of habit, but he had no distinct memory of having done so.

Above the waves of inebriation, one idea kept resurfacing: Sarah and the governor together, the sight of her standing in his hotel room, a sheet clutched up to her chin. Scoop felt a shudder of revulsion whenever he thought of it and the only way he knew to kill the sensation was to drown it in alcohol. How could she? What the fuck was she thinking? And how long had it been going on? The questions darted painfully through his mind. He thought of their bodies together, Sarah's and the governor's, lying side by side or one on top of the other or in any number of a dozen other positions his sadistic imagination forced to his attention. The very thought of them touching, of the governor's hands on Sarah's hips and thighs and breasts, made Scoop sick to his stomach. If it had been anyone else but the governor, Scoop told himself, it wouldn't have been so bad. If he had walked in on Sarah and found her with Earl or even with one of the Worthingtons—hell, even with *both* of the Worthingtons—it wouldn't have been as bad as this. But the governor? Jesus fucking Christ, how the hell could she be sleeping with *the governor*?

Images and sounds drifted in and out of his awareness. Scoop remembered lying down—he had no idea where or how long ago—

and Earl's face looking down at him from what appeared to be a great height. He was vaguely aware of the presence of Reginald and Bret as well, standing somewhere behind Earl.

"Scoop?" Earl had said. "Scoop, can you hear me? Are you all right?"

"Leave me alone, Earl."

"Scoop, we haven't seen you for days," said Earl. "Everyone's worried about you. Are you okay? Is there something wrong?"

"Please, Earl, just get out and leave me alone," said Scoop. He motioned in the general direction of the Worthingtons. "Take Leopold and Loeb over there with you."

Then slipping back into unconsciousness, back into the emotional anesthesia of alcohol. Scoop continued to drift aimlessly for days, weeks, maybe years. Until finally, one day, he was distracted by a painful ringing in his ears. As consciousness swam slowly into focus, he realized it was the telephone. He fought his way back to reality, back to the world of the living, and somehow the receiver found its way into his right hand.

"Hello?" he said weakly, for some reason surprised to find that he was still capable of speech.

"Scoop?" It was Reginald's voice.

"Yeah," said Scoop. "I'm here."

"Scoop, you've got to pull yourself together. We have a situation here." His voice sounded urgent.

"Situation? What do you mean situation?"

"It's about the governor."

"Yeah, no kidding. So what else is new? What about the governor?"

"He's gone," said Reginald.

At first the words didn't seem to make any sense. "What do you mean, he's gone? Gone where?"

"That's what I'm trying to tell you, Scoop. Nobody knows. He just disappeared. Nobody's seen him since yesterday morning when he dismissed his Secret Service agents."

"He dismissed his Secret Service agents?" Scoop's head was spinning. "Has anybody spoken to Pat?"

"Affirmative," said Reginald. "She hasn't the slightest notion where he might be. He evidently hasn't been in communication with

154

her in several days. Look, Scoop, I don't pretend to understand your odd behavior of the past two weeks. I don't know what's happening to you and maybe it isn't any of my business. But we have a crisis here and I'd like to think I can still rely on your support. Now we're going to be convening in my room in half an hour in order to discuss the situation. May I count on your attending?"

Scoop let loose a heavy sigh. "Yeah…yeah, sure, Reg. Whatever you say."

"Good. Oh, and Scoop, you might want to…uh, clean yourself up a bit. You've been a perfect mess lately."

Scoop hung up the telephone and made his way towards the bathroom, picking carefully through the obstacle course of furniture that, in his hung-over state, seemed to be deliberately veering towards him. He snapped on the switch on the bathroom wall and the overhead fluorescent light sent knives of pain stabbing through his skull. Squinting, he grudgingly glanced at his reflection in the mirror. It wasn't a pretty sight. His hair was matted; his face, pale and drawn. He wore several days' worth of beard growth and beneath each of his eyes was a dark semi-circle like a half moon.

Holy shit, he thought. Reg is right. I *am* a mess.

Pulling off his clothes, Scoop stepped into the shower stall and turned the faucet on hot, full blast. The spray of water stung his skin like a thousand tiny needles, shaking him loose, albeit slightly, from his inebriated daze. He stood under the shower for five full minutes, not moving, just letting the steady stream of water beat down on him like a hard rain. Then he quickly soaped his entire body, including his hair, and rinsed off. He toweled himself vigorously, combed back his wet hair, and pulled on a pair of pants and the only shirt he could find that smelled as if it might actually be clean. When he was fully dressed, he again surveyed himself in the mirror. He still wasn't going to get any offers to pose for GQ, he decided, but at least now he might be able to pass for human.

Well, what the fuck. Might as well have one for the road. He crossed to the bureau opposite the bed, poured himself a shot of Dewar's, downed it in one gulp, and headed out the door.

The meeting in Reginald's room proved to be a waste of time. Reginald, Bret and Earl spent close to half an hour proposing various unsubstantiated theories about where the governor might have gone to, but in truth none of them had a clue. Scoop sat wordlessly, sipping cold coffee from a white Styrofoam cup, until he finally lost his patience.

"Look, Reg, this is ridiculous," he said. "What the fuck are we doing here? We obviously don't have the slightest idea where the hell he's gone to, so what are we wasting our time for? I mean, do we know anything? Do we even know what time he checked out yesterday morning?"

"I appreciate your frustration, Scoop," said Reginald, trying for gentleness but somehow sounding condescending instead. "We all feel similarly. And, in point of fact, the governor didn't check out. If he had, I would have been notified immediately. He simply dismissed his Secret Service agents and left the hotel."

"Clearly he didn't wish for his departure to be noticed," added Bret. "He didn't even bother to take his luggage with him."

Scoop looked up sharply. "Are you saying his luggage is still in his room?"

"Yes, yes, Scoop, but don't get excited," said Reginald. "We've already perused his papers and there isn't a clue as to where he may have gone. Just a few pages of what I take to be the beginnings of an autobiography—which, if I may be so bold, is hardly destined to be a great work of literature by any stretch of the imagination. Why, the spelling alone is—"

"Reg, think for a moment," Scoop interrupted, a look of intense seriousness on his face. "Did you happen to see a brown satchel in the governor' s room? Like a leather attaché case, but old, weather-beaten?"

Reginald thought for a moment. "Why, no, not that I'm able to recall. Does anyone else have a recollection of a brown satchel?" Bret and Earl both shook their heads. "Scoop, do you have reason to believe it might mean something?"

"No, no," said Scoop. "I'm sure it's nothing. Still…you don't mind if I take a look myself, do you?"

"Not at all," said Reginald. He produced the spare key from his pocket and flipped it to Scoop.

Scoop found the governor's room in the same state of disarray it had been when the governor was there—papers and loose articles of clothing strewn about, a half-empty bottle of Jack Daniels still standing on the bedside table, sticky from spillage. Scoop paused for a moment before the governor's bed and felt a sudden shiver run through his body like an electric shock. Here's where it had happened, he couldn't help but think. Here's where their bodies had lain together. For a moment the images again flashed through his mind—the governor in his cowboy hat and boxer shorts, Sarah huddled naked behind a sheet. Scoop took a slug of Jack Daniels and shook the thought away.

He made his way slowly around the room, checking everywhere he could think of. All of the governor's other bags were in the closet, stacked up clumsily like a child's blocks. Scoop checked all of the drawers in the room and even under the bed, but the brown satchel was nowhere to be found.

Think. If the governor was really as protective of that damn bag as he seemed to be, he'd want to make sure no one got their hands on it while he was gone. So he'd hide it somewhere…somewhere it wasn't likely to be found. Okay, where? The options were limited. Where the hell do you hide something in a hotel room? Scoop suddenly became aware of cool air blowing gently on the back of his neck. He glanced up at the air vent in the ceiling.

Standing on a chair, Scoop tried turning one of the screws with his thumbnail. To his surprise, it moved easily. He unscrewed it and then the three others that held the faceplate in place. With that removed, there was now a black, rectangular hole in the ceiling. Scoop reached up through the hole and began feeling around. Nothing.

Oh, great, he thought. Just fucking great. What the hell am I doing? And I thought Reg was starting to lose it, searching for his goddamn hidden microphones. Any minute the maid is going to walk in and I'm going to have a hell of a lot of explaining to—

Suddenly, his fingers hit leather. Scoop grabbed hold and pulled. The governor's brown satchel came sliding out of the hole in the ceiling.

Scoop jumped off the chair and tossed the bag onto the governor's bed. Wiping dust from it with the palm of his hand, Scoop undid the buckles and reached inside. He pulled out the contents—a stack of newspapers and three books.

The titles of the first two books weren't familiar to Scoop. One was called *The Hoax of the Twentieth Century*. It appeared to be about the Holocaust. Scoop flipped through it and found several photographs that had been taken at Nazi death camps. The second book was called *Protocols of the Elders of Zion*. Scoop flipped through this one as well. There were lots of drawings, caricatures of people with long noses and horns and sometimes even fangs. The third book had had its cover torn off. Scoop had to turn back the first few pages in order to read the title. There was no mistaking what this one was about. It was an English translation of *Mein Kampf*.

Scoop turned his attention to the newspapers. Fairly recent, only the oldest of them had begun to yellow with age. Each of the papers was folded back to a story about the campaign and Scoop saw that they had each been marked with a red pen. One featured a smiling photograph of Lloyd Yeager and a death's head had been drawn over his face in red ink. In the margin, someone had written the words "motherfucker prick asshole." Scoop glanced through the rest of the newspapers. On each of them, the photographs of rival candidates had been altered and obscene comments had been written in the margins. Knives had been drawn on a picture of Al Washington, thrust into his eyes, and the words "die nigger" had been written beside it.

Scoop glanced again into the satchel. There was something he hadn't noticed before, a piece of cloth lying on the bottom. Scoop reached in and took it out. It was a red armband, decorated with a familiar black-and-white insignia. Scoop's body began trembling violently as he looked at the swastika.

You don't really know who my husband is. You think you know what you're dealing with, but you don't. You haven't the slightest idea.

Pat Stonewall's words rang in his ears as Scoop suddenly found himself overcome with nausea. He bolted to the bathroom and heaved vomit into the toilet.

If Scoop had found a severed head in the governor's bag, he couldn't have been more overcome with fear and disgust. All the childhood fears and memories of what his parents had told him about the Nazis flashed suddenly through his mind. Scoop had always suspected that the governor might not be completely sane. But he had never before realized how utterly dangerous the man was.

Until that moment, Scoop hadn't really cared where the governor had disappeared to or whether he was ever found. But now, slouched over the toilet, trying to catch his breath, his hands clutching white porcelain and his intestines squirming like a bucket of live worms, Scoop found that he wanted to know—needed to know where the governor was and precisely what he was up to. Finally, the obvious occurred to him. If Sarah and the governor were having an affair, she would be the person most likely to know his whereabouts.

Scoop pulled himself to his feet and wiped his mouth with one of the hotel towels. Weak from his vomiting, he staggered across the room to the telephone and punched in the numbers to Sarah's room. There was no answer. He tried the front desk.

"I'm sorry, sir," a man's voice informed him, "but Ms. Roman checked out yesterday morning."

Bingo. Scoop was willing to bet that wasn't a coincidence. So Sarah and the governor had left the hotel together. Maybe they were still together. But where? Scoop remembered Sarah saying she kept an apartment in Washington, her home base when she wasn't traveling on assignment. Maybe that's where they had gone? Certainly no one would think to look for the governor there. Scoop dialed the number for directory assistance in Washington, DC and asked if there was a listing under the name Sarah Roman. A mechanized computer voice, like something from a science fiction movie, read the numbers back to him. Scoop punched them in and heard Sarah's telephone ring on the other side of the country.

"Hi, this is Sarah. I'm not available to take your call right now, but if you leave your name and number…"

Scoop left a message asking Sarah to call him as soon as possible, then hung up. Of course, he knew that she probably wouldn't respond. After all, if Sarah was with the governor and she was trying to hide him, she would probably do everything possible to avoid Scoop. Well, what then? Was he just going to sit around, waiting for a telephone call that would probably never come? No, Scoop decided, there was only one thing to do. He would go to Washington himself, find Sarah, and confront her. He dialed the number of the agency that had handled their travel arrangements throughout the campaign.

"I need a one-way ticket to Washington, DC and a hotel reservation," he told the woman who answered. "For today."

"I'm sorry, Mr. Heidelman, but I'm afraid that's not possible," she responded. "Tomorrow's the Fourth of July. All flights from Austin to Washington have been booked for weeks."

"Look, I don't care how much it costs," said Scoop. "I don't care if you book me into the most flea-ridden flophouse in the city. I don't even care if I have to take a connecting flight through the *state* of Washington. Just get me on the next flight to Washington, DC."

Seventeen hours later, Scoop's plane touched down at Dulles International Airport. He rented a car and drove to his hotel, a run-down firetrap located in the inner city. Washington was in the midst of a brutal heat wave, the temperature already near ninety even at 8:00 in the morning, and Scoop felt his clothes sticking to his skin. He tossed his overnight bag onto the bed in his hotel room and immediately checked for the phone book in the drawer of the night table. There was a listing under the name Roman, with Sarah's telephone number and a corresponding address. Scoop scribbled the address on a sheet of the hotel stationary, then tried the number and left another message with his phone number at the hotel. Finally, he pulled off his damp clothing and sprawled across the bed. He had gotten little sleep on the overnight flight and the heat was making him feel groggy and unfocused. With the air conditioner in the window blowing cool air on his back, he dozed restlessly.

Four hours later, Scoop awoke with a start. He splashed cold water on his face, then tried Sarah's number again. Still no answer. Perhaps he had been wrong, perhaps she hadn't returned to Washington after all. Only one way to find out, he decided. He dressed hurriedly and took the stairs down to the hotel parking lot. The phone book had listed a Georgetown address under Sarah's name. Scoop drove west on M Street and then north where it intersected with Wisconsin Avenue. Down one of the city's many tree-lined streets, he found Sarah's address, an elegant, restored Colonial row house that, based on the multitude of separate doorbells next to the main entrance, had evidently been subdivided into a collection of individual apartments. Scoop found the doorbell next to Sarah's name and pushed it. A few moments later the lock clicked and the door swung open.

Sarah wasn't the least bit surprised to see him. "Hello, Scoop," she said flatly. "I've been expecting you."

"May I come in?"

Sarah shrugged and turned her back to him, leaving the door open behind her. Scoop entered and followed her up a narrow flight of stairs to a tiny, studio apartment—bedroom, living room, dining room, kitchen, all jammed into one small room. Sarah's luggage was scattered around the apartment, only half unpacked.

"You haven't answered my calls," said Scoop, then felt stupid for having stated the obvious.

"I didn't have anything to say," Sarah responded.

Scoop found it suddenly difficult to look at her. Instead, he glanced out the window at the tree-lined street below. "I need to know where the governor is."

"And what makes you think I know?"

"Oh, for Christ's sake, Sarah, because you're sleeping with him!" Scoop turned to face her. He had blurted the words out before he could think and there had been the unmistakable sound of pain in his voice—a pain he hadn't wanted to express, but there it was.

"And what if I am?" Sarah countered. "What business is that of yours? Really, Scoop, if I didn't know better I'd say you were jealous."

Scoop flinched at the very sound of the word. "Maybe...maybe I am. I don't know. I guess...I guess there were times when I thought that maybe we had something between us."

Sarah's face registered amusement. "*Us*? Scoop, there was no *us*. Really, now, did you think there was an *us*?"

Scoop lowered his eyes, unable to look at her again. He felt his face burning, but couldn't think of anything to say.

"Well, well," Sarah chuckled softly, "this is certainly a surprise."

"I just don't get it," Scoop said finally, looking up. "I mean, you and the governor. Not that it's any of my business. I know that. But I still don't get it."

"What's to get? I told you, Thurmond is a very complicated man."

"Oh, yes, Sarah. I'm learning that. I'm starting to learn just what a complicated man he is." The combination of anger and sarcasm made Scoop feel stronger, less vulnerable. He pushed on. "As a matter of fact, there are quite a few things about *Thurmond* that I'd bet you'd be very interested to know."

"Oh?" she said. "Like what?"

"Well, for starters, about the campaign itself. I mean the *real* motives behind the campaign."

"You mean the Worthingtons' scheme? Using the campaign to turn a profit?"

It was the last thing Scoop wanted, to lose the upper hand once again. But he couldn't disguise the total surprise he felt. "What...? How...?"

"How did I know?" asked Sarah. "Please, Scoop, I'm not a child. I've known about it for months. Thurmond told me. You didn't really think I could spend that much time that close to the campaign and not put two and two together, did you? I confronted Thurmond with it and he came clean."

"And...and that's all right with you?"

Sarah shrugged. "Why not? People run for office for one of two basic reasons: money or power. Sometimes both. What the hell. Thurmond didn't do anything that plenty of other candidates haven't done. He was just a little more focused about it. Really, Scoop, I don't see what the big deal is. You've been in politics your whole life. The last thing I expected from you was naiveté."

Scoop shook his head as if trying to wake himself from a bad dream. "Wait a minute," he sputtered. "Just hold on one goddamn minute. This doesn't add up. This doesn't add up at all. You *knew* about the plan? You *knew* the whole time and you didn't do anything? You're a reporter, for Christ's sake! The story of a lifetime gets dumped into your lap and you don't *do* anything?"

Sarah smiled smugly. "Sometimes we need to delay gratification for the promise of future rewards. Somebody said that, I think."

"Sarah, what the fuck are you talking about?"

Sarah sighed as if losing her patience while tutoring a particularly dense child. "Scoop, do I have to spell it out for you? Look, Thurmond wants to cut a deal. He wants to be guaranteed a role in any future Mondukis administration and he's got the influence to make it happen. That's where he is right now, meeting with the Mondukis people. And if Mondukis does get elected and Thurmond is granted a position in his administration...well, I don't have to tell you what that would mean to me as a journalist. I'd have my own personal pipeline to the White House. I mean, never mind fucking Profile Magazine. I'm talking my own network news show. Maybe even in prime time. That bitch Katie Couric will never know what hit her."

Scoop wasn't sure which shocked him more, Sarah's unbridled ambition or her willingness to express it so openly, without the slightest hint of embarrassment. He turned again to look out the window, trying desperately to collect his thoughts and sort out all the new information into some kind of sensible framework.

"And suppose," he said finally, turning back towards her, "I was to let the word out."

"About?"

"About you and the governor. I don't suppose he'd be nearly as popular with the voters if they knew he was cheating on his wife. Not to mention what a political liability he'd be to Mondukis."

Sarah flashed a look of scorn. "Don't be an asshole, Scoop. You haven't got any proof. Thurmond and I would both just deny it and you'd end up looking a fool. Christ, I thought you might actually be *happy* for me. Is that all our friendship has meant to you?"

"Friendship?" Scoop exploded. "*Friendship*?! *What* friendship? You used me to get to the governor, just like you're now using the governor to get to Mondukis. Friendship has nothing the fuck to do with it!"

"All right, that's enough," said Sarah. "I won't be spoken to that way in my own apartment. Now either you get out or I'm calling the police." She picked up the receiver and began dialing.

"Sarah, *listen* to me. You've *got* to listen to me. The governor has got to be stopped. He can't be allowed anywhere *near* the White House. Do you hear me? Sarah, please. You have no idea how dangerous he is."

"Oh, Scoop, *please*. Don't be so melodramatic. It doesn't become you. Look, I'm sorry I hurt your feelings, okay? I'm sorry I'm not the woman of your dreams or whatever the hell you thought I was. Now please just leave."

"Sarah, please, you have to list—"

She turned her attention to the receiver. "Hello, police? Yes, I'd like to report an intruder."

Realizing there was nothing more he could do, Scoop turned and left the apartment. Outside, the temperature had broken a hundred degrees and the intensity of the sunshine brought tears to his eyes. Although he didn't know it then, he would never see Sarah again.

From the time Scoop had met her, he had somehow believed that there was a tacit bond between them, that beneath their endless jesting and sarcasm they were actually kindred spirits, both hiding their vulnerability behind masks of cynicism. But now, for the first time in years, Scoop had finally dropped his mask. Only to find, much to his horror, that Sarah hadn't been wearing one.

On the way back to his hotel, Scoop stopped at a liquor store and picked up a fifth of Dewar's. Back in his room, he poured himself a tall glass and drank as if his very life depended on it. He finished the first glass and had just started a second when the telephone rang. Scoop answered it on the third ring.

"I hear tell you've been looking for me, boy," came the voice. It was the governor.

"Where are you?" Scoop demanded.

"That's for me to know, boy. Let's just say I'm having a nice talk with Mondukis and his people. Looks like I'm going to pull a little weight in his administration. Providing he's elected, of course."

"That wasn't the plan," said Scoop. "You know that."

"The plan wasn't working, boy. See, I got to thinking. Looks to me like no matter what you and those two little faggots did, the voters still wanted me. Well, far as I'm concerned, if the voters want me, they got me. You can't piss upstream too long 'fore the water starts getting mighty warm."

"Someone like you doesn't deserve to hold public office."

The governor chuckled. "No? And who the hell are you to say, boy? The way I see it, if the public votes for me, that's all the right I need. That's the beauty of democracy, boy. The people always get just what they vote for."

Scoop felt rage boiling up from the pit of his stomach. "Now you listen to me, you demented fuck. I know exactly what you are. I found your bag, the one you hid in your room. You remember, don't you? The one that proves what a sick bastard you are."

"Oh, yeah," the governor said calmly. "I almost forgot about my bag. And just where is it now?"

Scoop hesitated. "I...I have it here with me."

"Bullshit," said the governor. "You stupid kike bastard, you left it back at the hotel. I started to worry someone might find it, so I had Pat stop by and pick it up. It was right there on the bed, just where you left it."

"It doesn't make any difference," Scoop insisted. "I saw what I saw. And I'm going straight to the press with it."

The governor laughed. "And who the hell's gonna believe you? Everyone knows you've been tanked out of your fucking mind for the past two weeks. And when they find out it's all because your little girlfriend gave you the boot and you're under some kind of weird delusion that she's got the hots for me—well, no one's gonna believe a word you have to say."

"You fucking son of a—"

"You listen to me, you Jewboy piece of shit. You stay the fuck out of my way. Just go on and crawl back into that fucking bottle of yours and curl up and die. 'Cause if you get in my way, I'll crush you, boy. Crush you just like some kind of fucking animal."

There was a click and Scoop's ear was filled with the harsh sound of dial tone.

Trembling with anger and frustration, Scoop slammed down the receiver. But just a moment later he picked it up when the telephone rang again.

"Scoop? Is that you?" It was Reginald's voice.

Scoop took a deep breath. "Yeah, Reg, it's me."

"Thank goodness. I've been trying to reach you all afternoon. I called just a few moments ago, but the line was busy. Scoop, wonderful news. The governor cut a deal with the Mondukis camp. Mondukis is going to offer him the V.P. slot."

Scoop clenched the receiver tightly in his right hand. It was even worse than he had imagined. "The V.P. slot? Are you sure, Reg? Mondukis wants the governor as his running mate?"

"Absolutely," Reginald fairly bubbled. "It's been confirmed. Mondukis is going to announce it at the convention. And the best part is that the governor is going to take us all with him. We're all going to have positions in the new administration."

"We're all... Reg, are you sure? When did you talk to the governor last?"

"Early this morning. As I said, I've been trying to reach you. What's the matter, Scoop? You don't sound pleased."

"Nothing," said Scoop. "It's just that…this isn't what was supposed to happen."

"I know, old boy, I know. But we need to be flexible about these things. We can handle this, Scoop. It's a tremendous opportunity for all of us. Look, we can discuss all this when you get to Atlanta."

"Atlanta?"

"For the convention. We've already booked you a room. Look, I have to go. Just come to Atlanta, Scoop. Everyone will be there. We'll tie up all the loose ends then."

Reginald hung up, leaving Scoop alone once again with only his thoughts and his alcohol for company. Bit by bit, a plan began formulating in Scoop's mind. He remembered a few years ago, when he was working on another campaign, there had been this reporter for The Washington Post—a young, ambitious kid looking for his first big story. Scoop had taken a liking to him and had kicked some inside information his way. As a result, the kid grabbed his first front-page byline. In gratitude, the kid told Scoop that if he ever needed a favor, no matter what, Scoop could call on him. Scoop realized now that he couldn't even remember what the damn news story had been about. But he remembered the kid and the promise he had made and he remembered that at that time the kid and his young wife had just bought a home out in Virginia. Scoop wondered if they were still living there.

It would be an easy trip, straight down I-95 and straight back. Thousands of people did it every day. Scoop thought he might even be able to make it back by nightfall.

But it was already dark by the time Scoop made his way back into the nation's capital. Downtown Washington was jammed with Fourth of July revelers; as he drove through town, Scoop had to slam on his brakes several times to avoid hitting some of them. The temperature had dropped to the low eighties, but Scoop still found the air uncomfortably sticky. Many of the city office buildings were decorated with colorful flags and banners, and somewhere in the distance Scoop could faintly hear an orchestra launch into a medley of patriotic tunes as he pulled into the parking lot of his hotel. By the time he arrived back in his room, the traditional Independence Day fireworks had begun. From his window, Scoop saw them exploding brightly above the Potomac River, their booms echoing across the city like a mortar attack.

Scoop found the glass of scotch he had poured for himself earlier and took a drink. The liquor tasted suddenly repugnant to him. He dumped it in the sink, then poured the entire rest of the bottle down the toilet and flushed. No more drinking, he decided. Not now. He reached into the inner breast pocket of his jacket and removed the purchase he had brought back with him from Virginia. He held it up and examined it from all angles, like a child who has just found a previously unknown creature crawling beneath a rock.

Just come to Atlanta, Scoop. Everyone will be there. We'll tie up all the loose ends then.

Yes, thought Scoop. Yes, we certainly will.

The .38 revolver fit coolly in his grip.

14/ Georgia, July 18th

A s the Democratic National Convention opened in Atlanta, the
sky was heavy with storm clouds. It had rained for several days
before, a hard, driving rain that sent even the hardiest pedestrians
scrambling for cover and soaked the city streets until they were dark
and glossy like polished ebony. But as the first day of the convention
wore on, the rain ceased and the clouds grew progressively thinner
until, as if on a cue by the Democratic Party elite, the sun burst through
and the air grew warm and dry. By the second day of the convention,
the temperature had soared to nearly a hundred and the sun shone
brightly in a cloudless sky.

Scoop had an unnerving feeling of déjà vu. The flags and red-
white-and-blue banners, the signs and buttons and straw hats, the
brassy, overbearingly upbeat songs, the general air of excitement and
celebration—it was like the Fourth of July all over again. That's what
the national party conventions always reminded him of, as if all the
conventioneers had somehow slept through Independence Day and
were desperately trying to make up for it two weeks later.

Then again, maybe it was closer to a Hollywood premiere,
what with all the celebrities putting in appearances. Sharon Stone
was there to speak out against the exploitation of women and to
plug her new movie, a steamy erotic thriller called *Strip Search*.
Richard Gere showed up to lobby delegates for stronger language
about the environment in the party platform and also to urge more
leniency in the nation's motorcycle helmet laws. And Cher actually
addressed the convention, delivering a riveting speech on the subject
of homelessness—a topic with which she was very familiar, the
omnipresent press never tired of pointing out, because she had once
portrayed a homeless person in a movie.

When Scoop first arrived in Atlanta, he was greeted by two

pieces of news. For one thing, word of Mondukis having chosen the governor as his running mate had evidently been leaked to the press. Scoop reasoned that the leak had most likely been condoned by the party leaders, since it would head off the possibility of renegade Stonewall supporters staging a revolt during the convention. Probably it was decided that if the governor's delegates knew ahead of time their man was destined for the V.P. slot, they would keep their mouths shut and thereby allow the party to present a show of unity to the rest of the country.

The second piece of news wasn't unexpected.

"I feel simply awful about this, Scoop," said Reginald. "I hardly know what to say."

"Did the governor give any reason?"

"No, none. I pressed him on it, but he refused to elaborate. All I know is he doesn't want to meet with you. He told me that as far as he's concerned, you're no longer a member of the staff. He seemed quite adamant about it. I suspect he'd be furious if he knew I'd held a room for you. Really, Scoop, I don't know what's come over him. Did something transpire between the two of you?"

"No, nothing at all," Scoop lied. "I'm as baffled about this as you are."

Given their telephone conversation of two weeks previous, it was certainly understandable for the governor to have declared Scoop *persona non grata*. Unfortunately, it made Scoop's task all the more difficult. If the governor refused to see Scoop, if Scoop was banned from all future staff meetings—how the hell was he going to get close enough to the governor to kill him?

Now, on the third day of the convention, Scoop still hadn't found an answer to that question. He had spent the last two days wandering aimlessly through the hotel. Through the convention hall, alive with color and noise and the nervous excitement of deal-making, like the floor of a stock market where the commodity being traded was power instead of money. Through the rooms where the press congregated, the air thick with smoke and urgency and the sounds of rough laughter. Through the lobby with its continuous comings and goings, and the media shoving its lights and cameras and microphones into everyone's faces, each television station watching every move and analyzing every statement for some hitherto undetected significance, lest some rival station catch wind of an important trend or news item before they did. Scoop saw all of this clearly, saw it through eyes that were now no longer clouded by the blur of alcohol. And as he watched, he ran frequent scenarios through his mind, weighing and evaluating each one in turn, scenarios of how he could best get close to the governor with the intention of assassinating him. But most of all he waited, waited anxiously for his moment to arrive. This he did for two solid days and nights, all the while stone cold sober, obstinately refusing to partake of any substance stronger than black coffee. And after all that time, Scoop had managed to reach one and only one conclusion.

Sobriety was highly overrated.

"What do you want for lunch?" asked Earl. "Should we call that deli again?"

"Heavens, no," answered Reginald. "The sandwiches they sent yesterday were practically inedible. There was gristle on my roast beef."

"My tongue was fatty," Bret chimed in.

"How can your tongue get fat from eating a sandwich?" asked Earl.

"Not *my* tongue. The tongue they *served*."

They were sitting in Reginald's hotel room, Scoop and Earl and the Worthingtons. The television was turned to CNN and one of the network's correspondents was interviewing an enterprising young woman who had evidently discovered an original way to make a buck off the convention process by marketing colorfully decorated boxer shorts emblazoned with the names "Mondukis/Stonewall" to souvenir-hungry delegates. It was a sure sign of a slow news day, a desperate attempt by the networks to find an original angle amidst the information overload of the convention.

"How about Chinese?" suggested Earl, his forehead gleaming with perspiration. "There's that place on the corner. What's it called? Cat Chow?"

"Kong Chau," corrected Reginald, dabbing himself with a handkerchief. "And they don't deliver. Besides, they put MSG in their food. Damn, what the hell is wrong with that blasted air conditioner?"

"I've already called twice to have someone take a look at it," said Bret. "They claim they're all backed up. Why don't we just order pizza?"

"How do you know there's no MSG in the pizza?" asked Earl.

Scoop sat quietly in the corner as the conversation took place, continuing to evaluate his options. What if he could find out when Reginald and the others were planning to meet with the governor and simply burst in on the meeting? No, the room would no doubt be guarded by Secret Service agents. Scoop would never make it through the door. The governor hadn't yet arrived at the hotel, but Scoop had been able to ascertain which room he would be occupying when he got there. Maybe Scoop could somehow break into the room and wait for the governor's arrival? But no, that was no good either. That whole section of the floor had already been cordoned off.

"That's simply not the way it works," said Reginald.

"How do you know?" asked Earl.

"I just know, that's all," said Reginald. "No one puts MSG on pizza. It's only an ingredient in Chinese food."

"But why?" pressed Earl. "Is it Chinese in origin or something? I thought it was just a preservative."

"Actually, it's used in Chinese food as a flavor enhancer," Bret interjected.

"Then how come only the Chinese use it?" asked Earl. "Don't the Italians want their flavor enhanced too?"

There was just no getting around it, Scoop thought. Once the governor entered the hotel, there would be far too many Secret Service agents around for Scoop to even get close to him, never mind to actually pull a gun and get off a clear shot at him. What if Scoop could somehow get into the building across the street and shoot at the governor through a window? No, that was ridiculous. He'd need some kind of high-powered rifle for a maneuver like that and besides Scoop was no sharpshooter. Outside of practicing with the revolver for two weeks at a firing range near Arlington, Scoop had never fired a weapon before. Christ, did all assassins have this much difficulty offing their targets? Probably all John Wilkes Booth had to worry about was making sure he was at the evening performance instead of the matinee. And Lee Harvey Oswald hadn't had this much trouble getting around the Secret Service. Of course, according to some theories, he'd had everyone from the CIA to the Teamsters helping him out.

Yeah, great. John Wilkes Booth, Lee Harvey Oswald, and me. If my folks could see me now.

"I don't know, Earl," said Reginald, the exasperation rising in his voice. "Look, if you don't want pizza, just say so."

"It's not that I don't want pizza," said Earl. "It's just that some of the toppings you order are kind of weird. You know—eggplant, bean sprouts, broccoli."

"Broccoli happens to be quite nutritious," said Bret.

"I'm not saying that," Earl countered. "I'm just saying not everyone likes it on pizza."

Scoop glanced across the room at the television. CNN had interrupted the boxer shorts story for a news flash. The limousine carrying Mondukis and the governor had evidently been stalled in traffic three blocks from the hotel. On a whim, the two men had decided to travel the remaining distance on foot. CNN had a cameraman on the scene and Scoop saw the governor and Mondukis climbing out of the back of the limousine and waving to onlookers while the Secret Service agents traveling with the candidates scrambled to deal with the situation. The picture on the television screen was jittery, taken as it was by a handheld camera, but Scoop could clearly see the Secret Service agents dashing back and forth in the background, could see one of them talking excitedly on a walkie talkie, could see that they appeared to be panicking—panicking because they had found themselves faced with a scenario they hadn't anticipated and were therefore temporarily off-guard, undermanned, out of control.

Scoop felt a physical sensation like being kicked in the stomach. This was it. He would never get another opportunity like this and he knew it. Up until now, the assassination hadn't seemed completely real to him and hence he had been able to distance himself from his own emotions about it. But now the time had come, now there was no turning back. Scoop shivered. His entire body felt ice cold, yet he was aware of being bathed in sweat.

"Scoop, what do you think?" asked Reginald. "Do you want pizza for lunch?"

Scoop's breath seemed to be stuck somewhere in the center of his chest. Mechanically, in a trance, he forced himself to his feet and headed for the door. "Include me out."

"See?" said Earl. "I told you not everyone likes broccoli on pizza."

Scoop headed quickly down the hall to his room. His hands shaking, he fished the key from his pocket and fumbled madly with the lock. On his third try, the key slid in. He threw open the door and bolted across the room to the bed. Lifting the mattress, he pulled out the revolver and shoved it into the back of his pants, his belt holding it securely against his body. He threw on a dark-colored blazer to conceal the gun and dashed out the door.

Scoop hit the button to summon the elevator. He stood nervously, shivering, clenching and unclenching his fists, shifting from one foot to the other. "Come on, come on, come on." He hit the button again. *Where the hell was it? What the fuck was taking so long? Fuck it.* He darted through the door to the stairway and headed down the steps. He was moving so fast that he needed to grab hold of the banister in order to prevent himself from toppling head over heels down the stairs.

Five flights down, Scoop burst into the lobby. His eyes darted to the television that had been set up to broadcast non-stop news during the convention. Scoop saw that the governor and Mondukis were now only two blocks from the hotel. He weaved his way quickly through the maze of lights and television cameras, past the reporters and delegates and curious bystanders, and crashed through the front door of the hotel.

The heat hit him like a brick wall. He gasped for air. There didn't seem to be any breath in his lungs, but somehow he managed to keep moving. He ran, ran like he had never run before. From the corners of his eyes, he saw others running alongside him—journalists with notebooks, newscasters carrying microphones, cameramen lugging minicams—all racing down the street towards the two Democratic candidates. Scoop's heart pounded so fiercely in his chest it was as if he was being punched from the inside.

He ran. Past street vendors with tired eyes and disappointed mouths, hawking everything from hot dogs and soft drinks to balloons and disposable cameras. Past tourists and conventioneers, dressed in light summer dresses or striped poplin suits, their faces lit up with a combination of self-importance and amusement park glee. Past the city's usual inhabitants—the secretaries and executives and retail sales clerks—out for a walk on their lunch hours, their eyes shielded from the glare of the sun, their faces displaying mild annoyance at having had their city invaded by so many strangers. He ran.

Up ahead, Scoop could just begin to make out the figures of the two men walking towards him, surrounded by onlookers and reporters and Secret Service agents. Scoop's sphincter muscle contracted like a clenched fist up the ass. He was drenched in sweat now, as if someone had dumped a bucket of warm salt water over him. He sucked the air greedily, trying to pull some oxygen from the stifling heat. He felt dizzy, light-headed, as if he might pass out at any moment. His eyes burned with sweat and emotion. He ran.

Just a hundred yards away now and Scoop was able to tell which man was which. Mondukis was on the left, walking with an almost regal gait, smiling gently and waving, already seeming to adopt a presidential air. Stonewall walked on the right, his movements looser and more relaxed. He darted occasionally into the crowd to shake someone's hand or exchange a few words. He grinned broadly, clearly relishing the excitement and attention.

And still he ran. All at once, everything seemed to shift into slow motion. Scoop pulled closer into the governor's field of vision. At first Stonewall didn't seem to recognize him, just glanced in his direction and looked away. But then he looked again and the smile evaporated. An expression of surprise and mild concern slowly settled on his face as Scoop approached.

Scoop stopped just a few feet in front of the governor. His heart was hammering in his chest now and he was barely able to catch his breath. He reached beneath his jacket, behind his back, and drew the revolver. In one swift motion, he cocked the hammer and swung his arm in front of him, pointing the gun at the governor. There was a moment, probably only a split second but seeming to last an eternity, as Scoop pointed the revolver, but found that his arm was trembling too much to aim.

"He's got a gun!" Scoop heard someone shout.

There was no pain at first. All Scoop felt was a sudden blow to his chest, as if someone had dropped something heavy on him. The impact forced the air from his lungs and knocked him backwards. As Scoop stumbled, he pointed the gun wildly in the governor's direction and squeezed the trigger with every ounce of his strength. He heard the gun go off and his arm jerked spastically from the recoil as the sidewalk flew up to meet him.

"Oh my God!" a woman screamed. "He's been shot!"

Scoop blacked out. When he regained his senses a moment later, he was aware of being very warm and wet. He tried to lift himself, but found that he didn't have the strength to move. Summoning all his might, he lifted his head just slightly from the asphalt. He was surprised to find that there was a gaping hole, about the size of a fist, in the center of his stomach. His head collapsed back onto the sidewalk. A man leaned over him, a man wearing sunglasses and a dark suit, a man with a still smoking gun in his right hand.

Secret Service agent. Fucking son of a bitch. He had been shot by one of the goddamn Secret Service agents. Fucking bastard. *Fuck you, Fred.*

Scoop clung desperately to consciousness. Only one thing mattered now. Had he succeeded? Had he shot the governor? If only he had. If only the governor were lying on the same sidewalk as he, feeling the same sensations that Scoop was feeling—the sense of numbness spreading rapidly down his arms and legs, the increasing difficulty in breathing, the uncomfortable feeling of pressure as if someone were sitting on his chest. If only the governor were feeling these things too, it would be worth it, Scoop decided. It would make everything worthwhile.

Scoop was fading now, reality slipping in and out of his grasp. He was vaguely aware of hands on his body, of clasps being buckled and straps being pulled taut around him. He had a strange sensation of flying, of being lighter than air, and at once the thought occurred to him that surely this must be the end, that at last his soul had departed from his body, and that he would die without knowing the answer to the only question that mattered, the question that afflicted him far more deeply than any physical pain could. *No. Please not yet. I have to know.* Scoop suddenly realized that he was still alive, that he was not flying but being carried on a stretcher. He experienced an almost tangible feeling of relief, like none he had ever felt before. Then, once again, he was engulfed in darkness.

When Scoop forced his eyes open for the last time his vision was cloudy, as if he were seeing everything through a dense fog. He was in an ambulance, that much he knew, his arms and legs strapped to a stretcher so that he would be unable to move, even if he had possessed the power to do so. From somewhere to his left, he heard voices, harsh and urgent. Summoning all the strength that still remained in his ruptured body, Scoop twisted his head to the left to see what was happening. He saw that, in fact, there was another stretcher in the same ambulance, a stretcher alongside his own. Two paramedics were laboring furiously over another man, a man who had evidently also been shot.

"Shit," one of the paramedics said finally, "I don't think there's a hell of a lot we can do for this poor bastard."

A feeling of exhilaration shot through Scoop's body, bringing a wave of pain and nausea directly behind it. Scoop swallowed hard. It didn't make any difference. Nothing made any difference now. He had done it. He had killed the governor. That was all that mattered. He had done it.

Scoop looked at the blood-soaked body of the man lying next to him. Just at that moment, the ambulance hit a bump in the road. The man's head tilted slowly towards Scoop.

And in that instant, it all became clear. The feeling of inevitability that had been plaguing Scoop for months like a melody only half remembered suddenly made sense. Scoop saw it all, everything at once. He saw history spread out before him in all directions like a tapestry—past, present and future. And, more importantly, he at last saw his own place in that tapestry, saw the part that he had been assigned in building the future. He knew at last the role he had been destined to play in history, knew why all future generations of Americans would remember his name, and knew why that name would forever be linked with that of Thurmond Stonewall. Suddenly everything fit together, like the pieces of a puzzle, so that Scoop saw the picture whole, in all its detail and complexity. In the last moment of his life, Scoop finally understood.

And the last thing he saw, the image he would carry with him into eternity, was the sight of the cold, dead eyes of Senator Ed Mondukis staring back at him from across the ambulance.

The man he had shot.

* * *

The press was ecstatic. On what had been shaping up as a slow news day, the hottest story of the year had suddenly erupted.

More and more details would emerge in the media over the next few hours. The assassin had evidently been one Joel Heidelman, also known as "Scoop" to his friends. He had served as press secretary to Thurmond Stonewall during the governor's presidential campaign, but had recently been removed from that position. Heidelman was described by those who knew him as "a loner," having no family and very few friends. He was known to drink heavily, usually whiskey, and was evidently frequently depressed. A month ago, he had gone on a drunken binge while staying at a hotel in Austin, Texas. It was reportedly this episode which resulted in his dismissal from the campaign.

Heidelman had obtained the .38 revolver two weeks earlier in Richmond, Virginia. The gun had been given to him by a friend who lived in that state and who had purchased it there. Several people reported that they had seen Heidelman over the past two weeks practicing with the weapon at a firing range just outside of Arlington.

Heidelman had evidently brought the gun to Atlanta with the specific intention of assassinating Ed Mondukis, who had been the governor's chief political rival throughout the Democratic primaries. Possibly, by killing Stonewall's rival, Heidelman somehow thought he could regain the governor's approval, or at least that's what the psychologists were theorizing.

At any rate, both Heidelman and Mondukis were pronounced dead on arrival at Saint Joseph's Hospital at approximately 3:07 that afternoon.

Meanwhile, the convention was ablaze with confusion. Party leaders rushed to attend hastily called meetings while delegates dashed back and forth, speculating wildly amongst themselves. The excitement made the heat seem all the more intense. The convention hall felt like a tinderbox ready to explode, the air thick with the smells of tragedy and chaos.

Years later, there would be much speculation as to how it had actually started. Some would say it was a few delegates from Texas who simply got bored standing around waiting for something to happen. Others would say it was a group of hardcore Stonewall supporters who had been planning to stage some sort of commotion all along. Still others would say it really didn't matter how it started, that under the circumstances it was inevitable. Whatever the explanation, however it started, a chant slowly began growing throughout the convention hall.

"Stonewall...Stonewall...Stonewall..."

The chant grew louder and louder as more and more voices joined in. Until, before long, it had reached ear-ringing proportions, echoing off the walls and ceiling of the hall, reverberating through the very foundations of the building, like the simultaneous pounding of a thousand primal drums.

"Stonewall! Stonewall! Stonewall!"

And suddenly he was there at the podium, their last hope, their salvation and their savior, his arms outstretched to the adoring throngs below him. The crowd erupted, their cheers filling the room like the roar of the ocean as it crashes to shore. And the hall shook with the intensity of their devotion. For they were his people and he was their leader.

America stood poised on the brink of the future. It was a time of new beginnings, of a recommitment to the American dream. It was a time to rekindle the torch of freedom and pass it on to the next generation. It was a time for new leadership with new ideas. It was a time to put democracy back in the hands of true Americans everywhere. It was a time to celebrate the glory of a strong America, one nation under God, with liberty and justice for all. It was the dawning of a new age for America.

"Okay," said Reginald. "We can handle this."

Printed in the United States
98792LV00003B/133/A